THROWN

TABI WOLLSTONECRAFT

THROWN

Tabi Wollstonecraft

PART ONE
WAKE

CHAPTER
ONE

PROMISE

AMY

I stand near the edge of the cliff, the lights from Promise House making the long grass around my ankles glow pale yellow. I can hear the sea below as it crashes against the rocks with an angry roar repeated over and over in a hypnotic rhythm. This is how my Aunt Bethany died. She fell from a cliff during her nightly walk. Not here, not this cliff just behind her house. But somewhere close by. And now I am alone. All alone.

The people in the house are strangers. They were part of Aunt B's life here in Cornwall while my mother and I were living in the States. They know me only as "Bethany's sister's girl" or "the niece who went to America". Some of them say they remember me from when I was a child 'tearing through Promise House like a little whirlwind' and from the times Mom and I came over to visit Aunt B. But I don't remember them. I am among strangers.

Even Frank and his daughter Julie, the people I have lived with for the last six years - five of them with Mom and one on my own - seem distant. He isn't really my stepdad because he and Mom didn't get married but he's the closest thing I ever had to a father figure. And we both know that this is probably the last time we will see each other. We haven't said as much but it's the logical progression of things. He and Julie go back to Boston tomorrow and now that Mom is dead, there's no reason for us to have any further contact. The past year hasn't been good. Mom was our only link, the only thing we had in common.

In a way, Aunt Bethany's passing and leaving Promise House to me, her only relative, was probably the only thing that could have saved me from the downward spiral I had fallen into since Mom's death. The cutting had gotten out of control and I was sure Frank was going to send me to a psychiatrist, which might have even ended up with me being committed to an institution. It solved a problem for Frank too…the 'How do I get Amy out of my house now her mom is gone?' problem.

I look over my shoulder toward the big old house. The faint voices coming from there sound ghostly, drifting to my ears on the cool night breeze. I catch a woman's voice saying, 'Lovely funeral' and a man's earnest reply, 'Yes, but it's always a pity to bury people so young. How old was

Beth? Thirty five?' Someone replies, 'She was only thirty two. Much too young.'

I didn't cry at the funeral. I loved Aunt B and I loved visiting Promise House and exploring her rambling book shop in town but as I stood by her grave today and they lowered her coffin into the neat square hole in the ground, I just felt numb. I swear there's something wrong with me. Even the fact that I was standing next to Mom's headstone - she had put in her will that she wanted to be buried in Promise Cove where she grew up so her body had been flown here from Massachusetts - I didn't cry. I just felt dead inside. Dead and alone. I won't feel so dead later, after the mourners have gone home and everyone left in the house is asleep. I have a pack of razor blades in the night stand next to my bed and half a bottle of iodine and a roll of bandages.

I need to feel something. I need to know I am still alive and part of this world.

'What's up, Amy?

The surprise voice from out of the dark makes me jump and I let out a long exhale when I see Dell walking across the lawn from the house. She's my best friend and has been for five years. We lived next door to each other in Boston and became inseparable soon after we met, even though we were both fourteen then and that's an awkward age for girls to make new friends. Dell is short for Delilah. Delilah June. And despite her airy, spring-sunshine sounding name, Dell is a Goth. She wears only heavy dark makeup and long black clothes, although she sometimes adds an item of red or purple from her wardrobe. Maybe that's why we became friends even at the late age of fourteen: the outcasts stick together.

The irony is that while Dell looks dark and depressed on the outside, she's actually optimistic and funny. I may look normal on the outside…blonde hair, fashionable clothes and an easy smile…but on the inside I'm as dead as the vampires Dell likes to read about.

'Just thinking,' I tell her as she reaches my spot on the cliff.

She looks over the edge and takes a couple of steps back. 'Whoa. Maybe you should step away from the edge.'

I do. Not for the sake of my own safety but to make Dell feel more comfortable. 'I just needed some air.'

'Well, you don't want to catch two hundred feet of it on your way down to the rocks.' She cringes and half-closes her eyes. Her black eyeshadow makes it look like her eye sockets are empty. 'I'm sorry. That was a bad joke in the circumstances.'

'It's OK. How's it going in there?'

'Half the population of Promise Cove, which consists of maybe thirty people, is getting slowly drunk in your aunt's house and reminiscing about her. The most popular phrases are, "I don't know why she went walking on the cliffs at night" and "Thirty two is much too young to die." And there are no hot boys in there at all. At. All.'

'I guess I should get back in there.' I don't want to. I've had enough of being pointed at while they whisper, 'That's her niece who moved to America.' Or being told how great my aunt was. Or my mom. I know how great they were. I don't need to be told by strangers about my own family.

'Maybe it's time we started to wind down the wake,' Dell says, reading my mood.

'We're all tired,' I reply. It's been a long day and I still feel jet-lagged from yesterday's flight. A morning spent signing papers at Aunt B's lawyers, followed by the funeral and burial, and now this gathering at the house is overwhelming. Last week, I had no direction in my life. I felt like an unwanted tenant living with Frank and Julie and even though I had a job that got me out of the house every day, returning to a place I didn't feel welcome every evening was like a heavy rock threatening to pull me under the facade of my life into the depths of depression. The only person who saved me from actually drowning was Dell. She knew when it was getting bad and she would invite me over for a day or two.

And now I had my own house in Promise Cove, as well as a bookshop to run in town. 'A new start,' Frank had said when Aunt B's lawyers contacted me to tell me about the house and shop.

We reach the porch and head for the open back door. The warm light spills from the house, lighting up the grass in a yellow line that leads all the way to the cliff edge.

'Amy.' The voice comes from the shadows on the porch and both Dell and I start.

It's Frank. He's sitting on the porch bench. Is he in the shadows on purpose? Did he come out here to eavesdrop on me and Dell?

'I'll go inside and let you two talk,' Dell says, making a

tactful exit into the house and closing the door behind her. Frank lights a cigarette and the flare of his lighter illuminates his face for a moment. He looks tired. He took Mom's death badly, especially when he learned that her final wish was to be buried in the Sea Road Cemetery, Promise Cove, Cornwall, England. I think he took that as a slap in the face. She was leaving him in more ways than one. He pulls on the cigarette and the orange glow lights up his eyes as he looks at me.

'Amy, are you sure you're going to be alright here? On your own?'

So we're going to play it this way are we? The loving father figure who is concerned for the not-quite-step-daughter as she leaves home. We both know it's a lie.

'I'll be fine. I've got Dell to help me get settled then by the time she leaves, I should be in a routine.'

'She's only here for a week. You're going to get awful lonely out here by yourself. The house isn't even close to town.'

I look across to Promise Cove and the lights there. It does look a long way but Aunt B showed me some shortcuts across the cliffs and coves. I can walk there in fifteen minutes. If I take Aunt B's car down the narrow road into town, I can be there in five. I make a mental note to get her car out of the garage next to the house tomorrow. She had a silver Volvo the last time we visited, so I assume that is going to be my wheels from now on.

'I'll have the bookshop to keep me busy,' I assure Frank.

He lets out a little laugh which I'm sure comes out

more cruelly than he intended. 'What do you know about running a bookshop?'

'I can learn. I'm used to working.'

'Being a receptionist at a veterinary practice is nothing like running your own business, Amy.'

So, has he come out here to tell me I'm going to fail? Like I need any more discouragement. I feel scared enough about running Promise Books as it is. I owe it to Aunt B to do a good job and if I fail, I won't only be failing myself, I'll be failing her and that is the worst feeling in the world.

'I'm sure I'll make mistakes in the beginning but everything will be just fine,' I tell Frank.

'And what about...' he leans forward and the cigarette end brightens as he draws on it, casting his face in dark orange, '...your arms.' He nods toward my arms, which have been concealed all day beneath a thin black sweater worn over my funeral dress.

'They're fine,' I say flatly. I don't want to talk about this.

'Maybe I should find out your aunt's doctor's name. You should make an appointment.'

'I have the doctor's number in the house. If I need him, I will make an appointment.' I can feel my lips tightening as I speak. Stay calm. Don't betray any emotion.

He goes quiet for a moment as if thinking what to say next then he stands up. 'OK. I've said my piece.' Ah, so this is a little chat he feels obliged to have with me before he disappears forever with a clear conscience. He'll probably tell Julie on the plane back to Boston tomorrow that he tried to guide me and give me words of encouragement. Who will he be fooling? Her or himself?

'Our taxi comes in a few hours to take us to the airport. There's no need for you to get up and say goodbye. It's been a long day and you need your sleep.'

No need to say goodbye. Right. So let's just forget the past six years and pretend we don't even know each other.

'Where's Julie? I'll say goodbye to her now.' I start for the back door.

'She's already gone to bed,' he says, stopping me. 'As I said, we need to get up early for the taxi. Julie wanted to catch whatever sleep she can get.'

And not say goodbye to me, the girl she has lived with as a sister all this time? OK, maybe I was a pain in her ass the whole time, especially since I was five years younger than her and I demanded attention, but as that a reason to ignore me now? To go to bed and slip away in the early hours of the morning while I'm asleep? Surely I mean more to her than that. I shake my head in disbelief.

'Right,' I say tightly, 'well have a nice flight then.'

The back door bursts open and Dell appears, her green eyes wide, her mouth open. 'Amy!' She grabs my shoulders and I wince slightly as the one of the cuts on my right arm stings.

'What is it?'

'Remember I said there were no hot boys here?'

I nod.

'One just arrived. He's at the front door and he wants to talk to YOU!'

'What?'

She shrugs. 'I don't know who he is or how he got here but he is waiting in the driveway to speak with you. Now go, girl!'

'OK, OK, OK,' I say, catching some of her infectious excitement. I turn to say a final goodbye to Frank but he's gone and all that's left to say that he was ever there in the first place is his cigarette burning out in the long grass where he's tossed it.

CHAPTER
TWO

SHIFT

AMY

I make my way through the throng of black-garbed mourners in the house, noticing that Dell seems to have managed to reduce their numbers. I'm sure there were more here earlier. I'm tired and not in the mood to receive any more visitors, hot or not. Besides, Dell's idea of what makes a hot guy isn't always the same as mine. What could anyone want coming to the house this late?

The front door is open and the porch light is lit, casting a circular glow over the porch area. Beyond that circle of light, I can barely make out the cars parked on the grav-elled driveway and the dark silhouette of a figure standing with his hands in his pockets.

I squint into the darkness and cup a hand over my eyes to shade them from the glow of the porch light. 'Hello?'

He steps forward into the light and I actually have to hold back a gasp. He looks about my age, maybe older… maybe twenty one or twenty two. Differing opinions about what makes a guy hot are negated where guys like this are concerned. He must have all the girls of Promise Cove wrapped around his finger. His face is the kind you might see on the cover of a men's fitness magazine; ruggedly handsome with everything arranged in the perfect golden ratio of a work of art. His hair is dark and slightly tousled as if he just ran his fingers through it - and that thought immediately think that I'd like to run my fingers through it - and he has dark stubble on his cheeks and chin and neck that makes his drop dead gorgeous looks seem totally casual and natural. Like he can't help looking this good even if he hasn't shaved today and the cliff top winds have messed up his hair.

He's wearing a black leather jacket against the cool night breeze and beneath that a plain black t-shirt and black jeans with a black leather belt that has a simple brushed steel square buckle with an eagle design etched into it. His boots are black like everything else he's wearing. Is he here for the wake? I realize I can't ask him because I'm still holding my breath.

'Hey,' he says, shooting me a smile that makes me want to melt at his feet.

I exhale as steadily as I can and lean back against the brick wall of the house to make sure I stay upright. Dell could have warned me. OK, she did warn me by saying there was a hot guy at the door but she didn't say he was *this* hot. And she didn't warn me to fix my appearance before I met him. I run a hand through my hair self-consciously. I'm sure I must look a mess after standing outside on the cliffs in the sea breeze. 'Can I help you?'

'I know this is a bad time,' he says, indicating the crowd of people inside the house, but I thought I should bring your aunt's car back.'

I'm confused. 'Her car?'

He comes closer and leans nonchalantly on the strut that holds up the porch roof. He's tall and broad-shoul-dered with a slim waist and I wonder if he goes to the gym to work out or if he does some sort of martial art. I think it's the latter because his knuckles are bruised and have tiny scabs on them as if they've been cut recently.

'I was fixing the exhaust pipe for her. Put a new on on. The old on was hanging off.' He gestures into the darkness and I can just make out the outline of Aunt B's silver Volvo.

'Oh,' I say.

'Are you OK?' He looks me over and arches an eyebrow. Despite his leather and black denim, muscles and too-long hair, those gray eyes seem soft and honest. It's almost as if the hard man appearance is a disguise. No, not a disguise…more like armor to protect the vulnerable person I'm sure is hiding behind those eyes.

'I'm fine,' I say. 'Thanks for returning the car. Do I owe you anything? My purse is just in the house. I don't have a lot of cash but I can go to the bank tomorrow if you tell me how much…'

He lets out a low laugh and shakes his head. 'No, it's fine. I was fixing it as a favor for your aunt.'

A favor? For Aunt B? How did she know this incredibly handsome young man well enough for him to do her a favor and fix her car for free? What had she done for him? But if they knew each other that well, why wasn't he at her funeral? He definitely wasn't at the funeral; I would have remembered if he had been there. So what was his relationship with Aunt Bethany?

I don't ask him any of that. All that passes my lips is a confused, 'Oh, thanks.'

He laughs again. 'You're Amy, right? The heiress of Promise House?' The way he says it in his English accent makes it sound like an actual royal title.

I nod. 'The bookshop too. Do you read?' I close my eyes with embarrassment. What a stupid question. My mind had been working on how I might see this as-yet-unnamed guy again and the thought that had bubbled up from my subconscious had been that he could be a customer at the bookshop. My conscious mind had processed that infor- mation and turned it into the dumbest question ever asked by a girl to a guy she wanted to learn more about. Do you read? I shake my head at myself. Dumb. Totally dumb, Amy. Now he's going to think you're a freak and he's actu- ally right about that. You could have kept that part of yourself secret for awhile but now it's out.

He grins. 'Yeah, I read. I even have a literary name. Stoker.'

'Stoker.' I say it as if tasting it. 'Like Bram Stoker?'

'That's right. Except my name is Dean. And I didn't

write *Dracula*. My friends all call me Stoker.' He holds out his right hand, wanting to shake. They do everything so properly here in England.

I shake his hand. His skin is warm and his grip is strong and confident. His big hand drowns mine. 'Hi, Stoker. I'm Amy, as you know.'

He frowns at me. 'I said my friends call me Stoker. I don't know you yet so you can call me Dean.'

Yet? That word sends a little tingle through me. 'OK… Dean.'

He smiles. 'I'm kidding. Call me Stoker.'

I missed his joke because he threw me with the word 'yet'. I grin, which he probably thinks is because he was joking with me but is actually because he just mentioned the possibility of me getting to know him with a simple three letter word. And that possibility makes me feel happy even though I don't really know why. Sure, he's a good-looking guy but I've seen plenty of those and not been thrown sideways like this.

He lets go of my hand and says, 'You want to put the car in the garage?'

At the side of the house is a little garage where Aunt B always kept the Volvo and where I assumed it was all this time. I didn't know it was in the hands of hunky leather-jacketed Stoker.

He holds out the keys to me. Aunt B's keychain, a small silver "V" for Volvo, dangles beneath his hand. I take the "V" between my thumb and forefinger and pull and the rest of the chain and the key follow. I'm not sure I can touch him again and still breath normally. I've already made a bad enough impression on him. His presence on the porch is affecting me in ways I thought were just the stuff of romance novels. I feel like I'm drowning in his gaze and that I can't support myself without leaning against Promise House.

He steps off the porch and disappears into the dark. Letting out a long exhale, I push myself from the wall and follow him. 'I'll just open the garage,' I say, giving myself an excuse to get away from him for a moment. I need to breathe. I need to gather my thoughts into some semblance of intelligence before I speak to Stoker again. The garage key in on the same key ring as the car keys and I use it to unlock the garage door before pulling on the handle. The door swings up, revealing the dark interior of the garage. I find the light switch and flick it on. A wooden rack of shelves on the far wall holds an assortment of tools but apart from that the garage is empty. There's plenty of room for the car.

I gather myself, take a breath and turn to face Stoker. He's standing by the Volvo waiting. He's already done his job by delivering the car so why is he hanging around? Maybe he wants to see if my driving is as bad as my conversation skills. As I approach the car, I remember something about the Volvo and groan.

'What's the matter?'

'I just remembered, Aunt B's car has a gearshift.'

'Yeah, of course.'

'Over here maybe. But not back home. I've only driven an automatic.'

'You don't know how to work the gears?'

I shake my head. I could have tried to fake it and get the Volvo in the garage…it's only about twenty feet from here to there…but I don't want to risk damaging Aunt B's car.

He holds out his hand. 'Throw me the keys, I'll do it.'

Did he notice I didn't touch him when I took the keys from him? Is that why he wants me to throw the keys to him and not pass them to him? Maybe he thinks I'm scared of him. Thinks I'm taken in by the bad boy image he portrays. Maybe that's how most people see him…the bad boy? Or maybe he thinks I'm just a crazy American girl who doesn't like touching or something.

To prove him wrong on all counts, I walk over to him and place the keys in his hand, my fingers brushing his palm. He flashes me a smile that makes me wonder if he actually is a model and he slides into the car. He cranks it and guides it effortlessly into the garage while I stand on the gravel watching him. He climbs out and hits the light, sending the garage into blackness as Stoker reaches up to grab the door and slide it down.

As he reaches for the door, the t-shirt rides up his stomach, revealing a taut six pack of abs. Is he just perfect? He has the perfect face, body, smile and eyes. And what I've seen of his personality intrigues me. He didn't make fun of me when he could have and he knew Aunt B well enough for her to go to him when she needed her car fixed. Maybe I had to come all the way to England and start a new life to meet the perfect boy.

But that's the problem. If he *is* perfect…hell, even if he's just a nice guy…I need to stay away from him.

Because I'm broken inside. Far from perfect. He may think I'm a normal girl, despite the evidence I've given him to the contrary, but he can't see the darkness inside me. He doesn't know about the thin scars on my upper arms. He'd never guess that I'm the type of girl who keeps razor blades in her nightstand. That I need to cut myself to let out the darkness in the form of pain.

I think all this as he walks back over to me and hands me the keys.

'Well, thanks,' I say in a tone that suggests our transaction is over. He brought the car back and his favor is done. We are done. It's time for me to get back to the wake and for him to go back to wherever he came from.

And in the morning wen I wake up, the mourners will all be gone and Frank and Julie will be gone and Stoker will be gone.

I'll have Dell for another week but then she'll be gone too.

And Promise House will feel so lonely.

He detects me dark mood. He looks at me for a moment with those lovely eyes then he nods as if understanding what I'm thinking and heads across the gravel toward the narrow road that leads down into town. 'I'll probably see you around. Promise Cove is a small place.'

What is he trying to say? That I can't avoid him? Ever since stepping out on the porch, I've felt confused. He has done that to me. Somehow he has made me feel like I'm off balance and falling off a cliff into a raging deep sea. I stand there watching him leave and I don't say anything.

He reaches gate that leads onto the road then stops and turns around. He starts back toward me.

No, no, no…I want you to leave. Don't come back to talk with me some more. I'm not the pleasant girl you think I am. I'm not a sweet blonde American girl come here to run the bookshop and fit into the Promise Cove community. I'm the heiress of Promise House. The heiress of ghosts. The heiress of broken things and dark secrets.

Stoker reaches into his jeans pocket and pulls out a business card, which he places in my hand. 'If you want to learn to use the gearshift, I can teach you.'

The card is crumpled as if it has been in his pocket for a long time. The words 'STOKER AUTOS' are emblazoned across the top in stark black letters. Below that is a cartoon drawing of a crashed car and a list of services that Stoker Autos carry out. At the bottom, printed in smaller lettering is the name 'Max Stoker' and a phone number.

I arch an eyebrow. 'Max Stoker?'

'That's my dad. He owns the garage.' An unreadable look passes across his face. 'Turn the card over.'

I turn it over in my hand. Across the back of the card is a number scrawled in black pen.

'My number,' he says. 'If you want to learn the gearshift, just give me a call.'

He turns and heads back to the road, leaving me with his number and a head full of confused thoughts. I feel like throwing the card away. The last thing Dean Stoker needs is to have me enter his life.

But as I walk back to the porch and hear the hum of conversation from inside Promise House, I want to see

Stoker again more than anything I have ever wanted in my life.

Later when everyone is asleep I sit on my bed listening to the house settle. Creaking floorboards and pipes rattling in the attic and the wind blowing through the eaves. In my hand is a razor, taken carefully from the pack that now sits on my nightstand. The thin metal blade seems to glint in the light from the bedside lamp. Sitting beneath the lamp is the bottle of iodine and the rolled up bandage.

The mourners all left with their sentimental comments and pitiful glances and none of it seemed to mean anything to me. Of course not. To a girl who is dead inside, nothing can penetrate her being. Nothing affects her anymore.

What about Stoker? During the short time we spent on the driveway, I felt like he somehow got through a chink in my armor. I don't like that. Nobody gets to me that fast. Only Dell is allowed to get inside the shell I put between myself and the rest of the world and that's because she's my best friend and I've known her for years. No boy is going to turn up and sweep me off my feet. It isn't going to happen. I had boyfriends in Boston but even the longest relationship, which lasted three months, failed because I didn't allow myself to lower the armor. It's who I am. Nobody is going to change that.

I miss Aunt B. I miss Mom. This is the house where they grew up and I can feel them everywhere. I can imagine them as two little girls playing together, chasing each other down the halls and playing hide and seek in the rooms. I remember when I was a little girl myself and

Aunt B would set up treasure hunts that sent me off through the house and garden looking for the clues she had laid out. 'Look for the things that are out of place, the things that don't belong,' she would tell me to guide me toward the next clue.

There's only one thing here that doesn't belong and that's me. I don't know what I'm going to do when Dell goes back to Boston next week. I will be truly alone.

With Mom and Aunt B gone, the responsibility of the bookshop suddenly seems overwhelming, despite the false confidence I tried to show Frank.

It's time I felt something. Something intense.

I place the razor on the skin of my upper arm and without hesitating, I draw the blade across the flesh in a line that turns red with blood immediately. The sting makes me exhale through gritted teeth but at least I'm feeling something now. I take in a deep breath and position the razor blade a half inch below the cut I just made. I quickly make another and wince as the metal slides through my skin, parting it in a neat line.

I place the bloody razor on the nightstand and close my eyes, feeling hot tears spill down my cheeks.

'I miss you Aunt Beth,' I whisper. 'I miss you Mom.'

I start to sob, my chest hitching and my breaths coming out as gasps. Why did they leave me here? How am I supposed to go on without them? I can't do it, I'm not strong enough.

As the blood trickles down my arm in two perfect red rivers, I sob into the night.

MEMORIES

STOKER

The road winds down from Promise House towards town. I can be home in twenty minutes if I just follow it down to Main Street then take the hill road out of town that leads to our house.

I'm not ready to go home just yet.

The night air is cool and clears my head. I want to stay up here on the cliffs a bit longer, feel the breeze against my face, hear the sea crashing against the rocks far below. I scramble through the hedge that separates the road from the cliff tops. The hedge is supposed to make it safer for motorists and keep them from driving off the edge but if a car hit this tangle of thin branches and leaves, it would go right through and drive over the twenty feet of grass on the other side before tipping over the cliff and smashing on the rocks below.

The cliffs are a great place to walk and look out over the sea and forget about everything for a while but they are also deadly. A few people have met their deaths here over the past few years. Mainly holiday-makers who stray too close to the edge and don't know how fragile the rocks are in places. Once, a car did go through the hedge and ended up in the sea but the tide was in and the drunken lads inside escaped unhurt after swimming for the shore. I stood on the beach with a lot of other townsfolk and watched as the car was pulled out of the water by a mobile crane. An older man next to me muttered that strangers had no business up on the cliffs because they didn't know the dangers.

But what about Beth? She knew the area like the back of her hand, walked up here every night no matter what the weather was like.

And on a clear rainless night, she fell.

I reach the edge of the cliff and peer over at the sea below. The tide is going out, revealing the sand and rocks of the beach. I'm nearly three hundred feet above those rocks. To fall now would mean sudden death.

Just like it did for Beth.

With her gone, my future feels like its been set adrift on a stormy sea. Everything was so clear before but now I feel trapped. I can't see a way out anymore.

The girl at Promise House, Amy, was really attractive. I saw her at the funeral today but she didn't see me. No one saw me behind the trees. If my dad found out I went to

Bethany Anderson's funeral, he would kill me so I stayed out of sight. But I couldn't not go. Nothing could have kept me away. So I sat behind the trees and listened to the preacher as he said nice things about Beth and before it was finished, I slipped away.

I look up at the cloudy night sky. I was there, Beth. It was nice. A lot of people came out to pay their last respects. Rest in peace.

A tear blows across my cheek and I'm not sure if it's the wind stinging my eyes or if I'm crying. I sit on the grass and look out to the dark horizon and when I feel a second tear spring from my eye, I know it isn't the sea breeze.

I look across at Promise Cove, at the cluster of lights that shine from the houses, pubs and shops. This place is many people's idea of heaven on earth; a quiet town by the sea. For other people like me, its hell. It doesn't matter where you are or how idyllic your hometown is, you can't get away from the tragedies that have struck your life like cruel, unexpected lightning.

It doesn't make sense. None of it. At the cemetery today, before Beth's funeral, I visited Mum's and James's graves. I need to put flowers on them the next time I go. They seemed neglected, even though I go at least once a week. The flowers I put there die so quickly. I don't know how long it's been since Dad visited the graves. He probably doesn't know either.

Mum, James and Beth. All gone.

And I'm still here.

Even though I shouldn't be.

I rip up a handful of grass and throw it into the breeze,

watching it float out over the cliff edge and down to the beach.

There was a time when life seemed good and simple. When Mum and James were here, I could do as I wanted. Mum and Dad were focussed on my older brother and left me to my own devices. I spent a lot of time on the beaches just hanging out with friends and spending carefree days swimming and exploring the caves around the cove. Alone, I would sit on the cliffs for hours with my portable easel as I painted the cove or the sea or a flock of gulls. Or I would get a coffee in Sarah's Coffee And Cakes and sit at one of the tables, sketching customers for hours.

That time of my life seems like a half-remembered dream now.

For the past year, I have lived a secret life. Secret time at the beach waiting for dawn to break. Secret hours spent in the caves not for the pleasure of exploration and discovery but as an escape from the turmoil that my life has become.

Secret calls.

Secret jobs.

Secret visits to Promise House.

Maybe those visits were the only thing that kept me going after the accident. Gave me hope of a future.

Now that's all gone.

Why did I give Amy my number? Why did I say I'd teach her to drive her aunt's car? Am I so desperate to keep some connection to Beth that I'm going to try and make friends with her niece?

No, when I gave her the card, that wasn't in my mind at all. I liked her. She seemed a bit nervous but that could be because she had a house full of strangers and she was far away from home. It wasn't pity I felt for her, or a need to keep my connection to Beth.

Was it a sense of guilt?

No. Don't even go there.

I push the thought from my mind.

Maybe Amy will ring me and maybe she won't. Either way, I'll be seeing her again; Promise Cove isn't a large town and I know where she'll be working.

I feel my chest shake and I realize I'm laughing as I remember that she asked me if I read. I wipe the tears from my face and let the laughter come out. It sounds loud in the quiet night. If she saw the over-stuffed bookshelves in my room, she would realize how ridiculous the question was.

Maybe she'll see my room someday. Maybe I'll get to know her a lot better.

No, don't go down that route. You really think she'd be interested in someone like you? You think you'd be good for her? Of course not. No need to court disaster.

I stand up and brush the grass off my jeans before starting towards town. I stay on this side of the hedge and walk parallel to the road along the cliffs. It's slower this way but I'm in no hurry. Hopefully by the time I get back, Dad will be passed out on the settee. It's much easier that way.

A car drives by beyond the hedge, headlights cutting through the night as it takes the narrow road towards Promise Cove. The revs of the engine slow down and the red brake lights suddenly glow as the vehicle pulls over to the side of the road. I hear the metallic clunk of a door opening and closing. I stop in my tracks, frozen in place. It's almost midnight and I'm isolated up here. Why would the car stop? Did they see me from the road? It's possible the headlights picked me up as they turned the bend further up the road. So why stop?

I listen. The only sounds I can hear are the low thrum of the idling engine, a far off chanting that sounds like drunks staggering home from the pub in the cove and the beat of my own heart.

Then a voice cuts through the night. 'Dean?'

It's Dad. And even though he isn't the person I want to see most in the world right now, I breathe a sigh of relief and feel the tension in my body relax. I walk across the grass to the hedge. He's standing next to the Astra, leaning on the roof as if to steady himself, squinting at me. 'Dean, is that you?'

'It's me, Dad,' I say, climbing through the hedge. I have no doubt he's been drinking…by midnight he's usually passed out…but drinking and driving is a new one for him. We don't have many police around here and the nearest police station is in Penzance but he could still hurt himself or someone else driving around under the influence.

'You didn't come home,' he says, 'so I came looking for you.'

'You didn't have to do that, Dad.'

He nods too emphatically, his actions exaggerated by alcohol. 'Yes, yes I did. But I didn't have to look very far. Do you know why?'

'Why?' I walk around to the driver's side of the car. No way is he driving home in the state he's in.

'Because I knew you wouldn't be able to stay away. It's her funeral today. You've been to her house, haven't you?' He narrows his eyes accusingly.

'I was just walking on the cliffs, Dad. Give me the keys, I'll drive us home.' I hold out my hand.

He looks at me and furrows his brows then tosses the keys at me. I catch them and he staggers around to the passenger side. He's had a lot to drink, I can tell from his movements and the way his eyes are heavy-lidded. He's damn lucky he didn't kill himself. But then he's probably past caring about that anymore. Mum and James are gone and I'm not the son he wants me to be. I'm just one more disappointment in his disappointing life. In fact, I'm probably the biggest disappointment for him.

I slide into the driver's seat and he clambers into the passenger seat and I pull out into the road, casting a sideways glance at him every now and then. He's sitting forward slightly, his head drooping against his chest. He smells of alcohol and sweat and motor oil because he's still wearing his overalls from the garage. He didn't even bother to get changed, just got home and started drinking.

He mumbles something but it's so low, he must be talking to himself. His eyes are closed so maybe he's asleep and dreaming. 'What did you say, Dad?' I ask quietly.

'Shouldn't go walking along the cliffs at night. Anything could happen.'

'I'm OK.'

'You're OK but she isn't. She isn't OK at all.' His head

droops further and a tear falls from his face to join the grease stains on his overalls. He always gets like this when he's drunk. It's pitiful to watch him drink himself into a pit of sorrow every night and cry his heart out. Sometimes he cries himself into unconsciousness. Occasionally he turns violent. I prefer the unconsciousness.

I don't reply to him. He misses Mum and James. We both do. No need to exacerbate the situation by talking about it with him because he's already lost in his own thoughts and heading down the path to despair. Anything I say can only move him along that path more quickly or make him lash out at me. So I stay quiet and concentrate on the road ahead as it takes us into Promise Cove.

The shops and pubs of Main Street slide past the window and in the light from their windows seeping into the car, I can see that Dad is asleep, his tears drying on his cheeks. As I take the road out of town that leads to the garage, my mind slips again to Amy Anderson. I keep thinking about her standing on the porch of Promise House in her black dress, her blonde hair blowing slightly in the sea breeze. She's attractive for sure but I think my attraction to her goes beyond her looks. When I saw her standing there in front of the big house, I got the sense that she was as lost in life as I am. Her vulnerability seemed to surround her like a shimmering aura. I don't know much about her apart from the fact that she is Beth's older sister's daughter and they moved to America when Amy was young. Beth mentioned her a few times and said Amy wrote poetry and stories and one day I might see a book by her in Promise Books. Beth also told me that her sister's grave isn't in America at all but is in the Sea Road Cemetery, close to where Mum and James are buried.

Beth was Amy's only living relative. And now she's gone. So Amy is alone in the world. Like me.

I pull into the forecourt of Stoker Autos and drive past the garage's Reception doors to the stairs that lead up the side of the building to the door of our house on the second level. There's no way I can get Dad up there while he's asleep.

'Dad,' I say, shaking him a little.

He stirs but doesn't reply.

'Dad,' I say louder.

He opens his blurry eyes. 'What? What is it?'

'We're home.'

He squints out through the windscreen.

'So?'

'So you need to get upstairs and to bed.'

He lets out a whiskey-ridden sigh and opens his door. I climb out and get around to the passenger door before he falls out onto the concrete. As I pull him up and hook his arm around my shoulder, I grab his waist and lead him to the foot of the stairs. He looks up to the door on the second floor.

'That's a long way up.'

'Come on, we can do it.' I start up the stairs, half-dragging, half-supporting him. He leans heavily against me and we get to the door after a few minutes of clumsy manoeuvring and staggering. I dig my keys out of my pocket and unlock the door. As soon as it opens, Dad stumbles inside and makes it to the settee before falling face down onto the cushions, one arm hanging over onto the floor. He's already snoring.

There's no point trying to get him to his bedroom now so I take off his boots and place them neatly on the floor under the coffee table. I arrange the cushions so they're supporting his head like a pillow and I go to his room to grab the blanket from his bed.

As I open the door to his room, I see the scattering of photos on his bed. He's taken the shoebox of photographs from the back of his closet where he keeps it and he's pulled out handfuls of pictures and laid them out on the sheets. The ones he's taken out are mainly of him, Mum and James. I'm in a few but only incidentally. The photos of just me or where I feature prominently are still in the shoebox.

I pick a picture up and even though its dark in the bedroom, I don't need to see the photograph clearly to know exactly what it looks like. I can still remember the day it was taken. James was playing football for the Penzance Pirates and they had just won the league thanks to him. In the photograph, he's being held aloft by his teammates, all of them wearing the Pirates blue and green football shirt. James was twelve when this was taken. I'm standing in the background, among all the other support-ers, ten years old and looking at my brother like he's my biggest hero.

I place the photo in the shoebox along with all the others after I gather them up from the bed and I put the box back into the closet where it belongs. Pulling the blanket from the bed, I return to the living room and drape it over Dad gently. He has a bad enough time dealing with the memories already without getting out old photos to torture himself even more.

He left my photos in the shoebox because no matter what I do, I will never be James. My older brother was everything Dad wanted in a son. He was good at sports, a hit with the girls and everything a real man should be in my dad's eyes.

When I was growing up, it was always in James's tall shadow and even though I tried to please Dad there was nothing I could do that was good enough for him. My interests didn't involve sports. I was more creative, something my dad never understood. As I got older, I became more insular and spent a lot of time alone drawing and reading. Even my exercise routine was the polar opposite if James's. He went to the large gym in Penzance where he was popular with all the other customers. I spent the money I saved up from working at a boat hire firm in the summer on a set of weights which I used diligently in my room.

I always tried to emulate James because he was my hero but I could never do anything as well as he did.

And my father hated me for it.

And now that James is gone, Dad seems disgusted that it wasn't me who died in the car that day. If he could trade me for James, put me in the grave at the Sea Road Cemetery and have his favorite son back, he would do it in a heartbeat.

I leave him sleeping on the settee and I go to my room. Even my familiar belongings can't calm me down. Old paperbacks, most of them bought at Promise Books, stuff the shelves from floor to ceiling and on a small table in the corner, my paints and sketchbooks and pencils sit waiting like old friends.

On the easel at the foot of my bed is an unfinished oil painting of the beach and cliffs at Carbis Bay. I drove out there last week early in the morning and caught the scene just as the sun was rising. My painting hours are all stolen moments away from Dad and the garage.

He hates me doing anything creative, even reading. It reminds him that the son he has left on this earth is nothing like him. Nothing like James.

The room feels like it's shrinking in on me and I suddenly have to get out. There's a rage building inside me and I know that there is only one way to release it, to get it out of me before I go mad. I pull open my door and storm past the sleeping figure of my father, back down the steps and to the car.

When I pull out of the garage and into the road, I'm already hitting fifty miles per hour. On these roads, that's dangerous.

But by now I'm past caring.

Now, danger is my friend.

———

There are three of them coming out of the pub, three men in their early twenties. A group of girls walking in front of them could be the reason the men came out. They're wolf-whistling the girls and I hear one of them shout, 'Get your tits out." Perfect.

I stand in the alley…in the shadows…among garbage and overflowing dumpsters. The Astra is parked across the street in the darkness by a closed restaurant. I drove twenty miles out of Promise Cove to get here and every mile on the winding roads just made my fury twist my gut. I don't know why I get this way and at the moment, I don't even care. I just know what has to be done.

The street is dark. Only a warm glow emanating from the pub windows casts any light anywhere. The clouds have covered the moon as if nature is aiding me in my dark deed. They're approaching slowly, the girls are walking rapidly with their heels click click clicking on the pavement but the boys are falling back, lighting cigarettes and laughing and passing crude remarks about the girls.

As the girls pass the mouth of the alley, I melt back into the shadows. A shout from along the street reaches us. 'Wait for us, girls! We've got something for you.'

The girls click past, obviously in a hurry to get away from these jerks. They don't see me.

After they've gone past and I can hear the three young men approaching, I step out onto the pavement.

They are ten steps away from me. They all see me and stop. One of them grins.

I don't say anything. I don't need to provoke them. For drunken low-life like this, I don't need to communicate with them verbally for them to know the situation.

Three of them.

One of me.

Dark night in a quiet street.

This is what they live for.

And right now, this is what I need.

'Hey you,' one of them says, 'what did you say to those girls?'

It usually starts like this. They make up some justification for what's going to happen next. I don't know why they bother.

The one who spoke is the tallest, maybe six two. He's wearing low-slung jeans and a t-shirt like his mates but his t-shirt is tight and shows off a barrel chest and big arms but also a paunch around his mid-section. His head is shaved and he wears a single gold stud in his ear. Tattoos down both arms. I know the type; too many hours in the gym doing bench presses and bicep curls to make his upper body big. He's big alright. And probably slow.

The one standing in the middle looks like a wannabe Hell's Angel but without the bike and without the strength to back up his attitude. His t-shirt is black with a white skull design on the front. His belt is studded with chrome points. Also shaven-headed, he sports a goatee and a few trophy muscles from misspent time in the gym.

On the end stands a thin wiry dark-haired man who will probably cause me the most trouble. Already, his fists are opening and closing over and over, flexing the tendons while his knuckles crack.

Tall Boy comes at me first, all pretence of me saying anything to the girls forgotten or not mattering anymore. He takes a swing at me. I block it with my forearm and drive a fist into his face. He lets out a surprised 'whooofff' and staggers back, leaving room for Wannabe to lash out at my head. His fist lands behind my ear, which probably hurts him more than it hurts me as his fist cracks on my skull. He cries out and I hit him with a right hook that sends him sprawling into the gutter.

Wiry surprises me by stepping back slightly, letting his mates do the work. Is he sizing me up or is he scared?

Wannabe comes running at me, probably hoping to barrel into me and pin me against the brick wall behind me. I sidestep and connect my fist with his belly as he reaches me. He collapses to the pavement, writhing like a pinned insect.

Tall Boy looks at Wiry. 'Come on, Mike, let's both rush him.'

Mike nods and they come at me together. I duck below their swinging fists and drive my own into Mike's solar plexus. I overestimated him earlier. The way he came swinging at me opens him up to me and I have choices of where I want to hit him. I hammer a fist into his face and he goes down.

Tall Boy sees his two friends on the ground and decides enough is enough. He turns and runs. Fine. Let him go.

I walk across the street and get into my car. As I drive past them, they shout obscenities at me but I can't hear the words because my ear is still ringing from the blow I received.

I drive out of town and take the road back to Promise Cove. My headlights cut through the night and I drive back calmly. Just before the cliff road that leads into town, I take a dirt road to the sea. There's a little cement parking area near the dark beach. I park the Astra and get out, already pulling at my clothes and leaving them on the ground.

By the time I get to the water's edge, I'm naked and all my clothes are strewn across the sand behind me.

It's cold. Very cold. My flesh prickles as I wade in up to my waist then dive forward, hearing the rush of water in my ears as I go under. I force myself down, down into the cold depths until I touch the bottom.

Lying there and holding my breath until I almost black out, I feel the rhythm of the sea all around me. It moves ceaselessly to that rhythm all the time, no matter what is going in our lives. The sea simply follows its own internal rhythm. And as we live out our short lives, it goes on like this forever.

My lungs scream for air and I slowly float to the surface, taking in a deep gulp of the sweet night air as I break through the gentle waves. I tread water for a moment, looking at the cold dark water around me as it holds me up in its dark embrace. Then I swim to shore and crawl out onto the sandy beach.

I curl up on the sand among the shells and the pebbles and I remember a night like this when I crawled out of the sea and collapsed on a beach. That night, I lost everything.

I let my tears mingle with the saltwater on my face and I lay beneath the cloudy night sky and weep for what was lost.

CALL

AMY

The alarm on my phone drags me from a deep sleep and a dream where I was standing on the edge of a cliff losing my balance and about to fall. I don't even remember setting the alarm on my phone. What time is it? I squint at the screen. Eight thirty. I switch off the alarm and bury my head back into the pillow as I replace the phone on the nightstand. Too early. Too tired.

I try to get back to sleep but part of me is afraid that if I do drift off, the nightmare will return and this time I might actually fall off the cliff. I heard a myth once that if you die in a dream, you die in real life. It sounds lame but my brain won't let me go back to sleep to test the theory out. I sit up and check the wounds on my arm, gingerly pulling off the bandage. It comes away bloodied but the two lines across my arm aren't bleeding anymore. They are pink and stand out against the lighter scars that criss cross my skin. Some of those scars go back years.

I throw the bandage into the trash can across the room and slide my legs over the edge of the bed. Eight thirty. Frank and Julie will be long gone. I wonder if they sneaked out as quietly as they could so they wouldn't wake me and have to be subjected to a goodbye. I wonder if I will ever hear from them again. I doubt it.

My suitcase is sitting on the floor at the end of the bed. I open it up and pull out underwear, jeans and a thin black sweater. After putting them on, I scrape my hair back and use a black hair band to keep it in place. This bedroom has its own bathroom so I use it and brush my teeth before opening the door to the upstairs hallway.

The mouth-watering smell of eggs and bacon assaults my senses and I hear Dell clattering about in the kitchen downstairs. I take the stairs two at a time, holding the railing tightly because even though I'm in a hurry to see my friend and eat breakfast, my socked feet slip too easily on the polished wooden steps. I cross the hall to the kitchen and open it to see Dell wearing a green apron that has the words 'Kiss The Chef' embroidered across it over her jeans and black t-shirt. She's wearing light makeup at the moment but I know that's because it's early and I'm the only person who's going to see her. Later, she will put on her trademark heavy Goth eyeshadow and dark lipstick. She never leaves home without it.

She has two plates on the counter and is using a

spatula to toss bacon out of the frying pan onto them. There's already scrambled egg on the plates and toast in a little metal rack on the table by the window. I don't know what I'm going to do without Dell. I really don't.

'Hey, you,' she says as she sees me.

'Hey. Anything I can do to help? It smells delicious.'

'Just take a seat and I'll bring everything over. Yesterday was a tough one so I'm going to make my best friend a home-cooked breakfast to cheer her up.' She takes sausages from the oven and adds them to the plates then brings everything over. 'And since we're in England, I made us a post of tea.' She indicates a chrome tea pot and two cups with saucers.

'This looks amazing!' The smells drifting up from my plate make me realize how hungry I am. I ate barely anything yesterday.

'Well we bought way too much food at the grocery store yesterday when we thought Frank and Julie would be staying for breakfast. Shame to let it go to waste.' Dell removes the apron and sits down opposite me at the table. I can see why Aunt B set the table here; the window looks out over the cliffs to the sea with a view of Promise Cove in the distance. It's already sunny out and the sky is a vivid deep blue.

'Speaking of amazing,' Dell says, taking a bite of a sausage, 'have you called that dreamy Stoker boy yet?'

'You know I haven't. Probably not going to either.'

She rolls her eyes. 'It's almost nine o clock. By nine thirty, a boy that hot will be taken. You don't want some

English girl to beat you to the prize. So you have a half hour to figure out what you're going to say to him.'

'I'm not calling him. For all I know, he's already taken. This breakfast is delicious!'

'Stop trying to change the subject. If he was already taken, he wouldn't have offered to help you with your aunt's car.'

I shrug. 'He was probably just being polite. Aren't all English people polite?'

'Polite? Honey, he wants to take you for a ride.'

'Dell!'

She puts her fork down and chews on a piece of bacon. 'The fact is, we need the car. We're going to go to the bookshop today, right? Then we need the car.'

'Yes, we are going to the bookshop today…we're going to walk.'

'Walk? I don't do "walk". Call Stoker.'

'If you don't do "walk", then you should learn to drive. I don't know how you survived in Boston without being able to drive.'

She smiles and flutters her eyelashes comically. 'I had my best friend to drive me. And there are buses in Boston. I don't think there are any buses here.'

'There are buses. Not like in Boston but there are buses.'

'Can I catch a bus that will take me from the end of the driveway to the bookshop?'

'No.'

'Then we need the car.'

'You are so lazy, Dell.'

'Lazy? Or deserving of being pampered?'

'Lazy.'

'Just call the hot boy and let him show you how to handle the stick.'

I almost choke on my scrambled eggs. 'I bet it took you all night to think up that double entendre.'

'No, it just came to me in a flash of inspiration. There are many more were that came from. How about…'

'Dell, we are walking into town today no matter what your filthy mind comes up with.'

She looks out of the window and purses her lips in a fake pout.

'And I'm not calling Stoker,' I add.

She folds her arms across her chest like a petulant six year old and continues looking out of the window.

I laugh. 'You really are crazy, you know that?'

'Takes one to know one.'

'Well these two crazy girls have a bookshop to open. Promise Books has been closed for more than a week. We don't want to lose out on business.'

'Here? In Promise Cove? Where else are they gonna go to buy books, hmm? It probably takes three weeks for an online store to deliver all the way out here. If they want books in this town, you're it.'

'Well then we have the demand so let's open up the supply.'

'Fine,' she says, 'I will walk. But just this one time. Tomorrow you drive, whether you can work the gears or not. I'd rather die in a car crash than collapse from exhaustion. It's a much quicker way to go.'

I look out of the window at the bright day. I'm actually looking forward to the walk. The house has a lot of memories from my childhood drifting around within its walls like ghosts. They're happy memories of my mom and Aunt B but the fact that both of them are gone now puts a tinge of sadness on everything I think about. Maybe some fresh air will clear my head. And I know that despite her protests, Dell wants to see Promise Cove and the bookshop too.

'I need a half hour to do my makeup,' she reminds me. 'And remember, in that half hour some Promise Cove floozy will probably make a move on poor Stoker and he'll be helpless before her charms.' She makes the "call me" sign with her thumb and pinky and mouths, 'Call him.'

I pick up the apron and throw it at her but she's already scooted out of the kitchen and the apron his the cupboards behind where she was standing.

'Missed,' she says and I hear her ascend the wooden stairs to her room.

I go to the key hooks in the hallway and take the bookshop key, which has a green vinyl key tag in the shape of a stack of books. Aunt B did like her key tags and chains. I put the key into my pocket and listen to the silence of the house. The only sound is Dell clattering around in her room.

Soon she'll be gone back to Boston and I'll be here in this house alone with only the ghosts for company.

———

By the time we reach the bookshop, Dell has stopped complaining about her feet and fallen into a sullen silence. I'm filled with a sense of dread that feels heavy in my stomach. Main Street is busy with locals and people on vacation and as we walk past the stores and pubs toward Promise Books, I can feel they eyes of the locals on us. I know that small towns like this can be very wary of strangers so what must they think of this American girl coming here to run Promise Books? My aunt was well-liked in Promise Cove but she lived here all her life and although I was born here and spent the first five years of my life here, I am a stranger to these people. It reminds me of a scene in a comedy horror movie I saw once where two American brothers go into a village pub in England as as soon as they step through the door everything goes silent and everyone turns to face them. That's how I feel now, like I'm being scrutinized be everyone. I don't like it. I don't like attention at any time and I don't need it now that I'm worried about my own ability to keep Promise Books running. I have enough to worry about without everyone staring.

The bookshop has a closed sign hanging inside the door and dark green blinds are pulled down behind the windows. It's just as Aunt B left it the evening she locked up, never knowing that she would be falling from the cliffs to her death that night and wouldn't be opening up again the next morning.

I push the key into the lock and turn it. A satisfying click comes from the lock and I push the door open, imme-diately smelling the familiar pulpy smell of the book inside. A bell attached to a leather strap rings as the door opens. Dell follows me inside and I close the door behind her. I feel better now that we're in here away from the prying eyes but I know the door can't remain closed. The whole point of the store is that we get customers.

'Wow, look at this place,' Dell says, eyeing the stacks and shelves. 'And it smells great.'

I pull the blind on the main window and it rolls up, letting in a stream of sunlight that reveals the dust motes in the air as well as the interior of the shop. Every wall is packed with books and a six feet tall bookshelf runs down the center of the shop, stuffed with books on both sides. Hand-written labels taped to the shelves denote genre and author names alphabetically. A counter to the left of the door holds a display of bookmarks and the cash register. On the wall behind the counter is a watercolor painting of the bookshop which I've never seen before. A swivel seat upholstered in green fabric sits behind the counter and a door at the far end of the space behind the counter leads to a small kitchenette and a bathroom beyond that. I remember Aunt B making a cup of tea for herself and getting juice for me from that kitchenette when we would come to visit from Boston when I was younger.

The last time I was here was a year ago, the day after Mom's funeral. Aunt B made us coffee and as we sat drinking it behind the counter, I asked her if I could come live with her. She said she wanted me to but I had to finish school in Boston. Frank had said that was fine and the plan had been that I would come here after finishing.

But at that time I was too depressed to do anything

with my life other than commit to the daily routine of going to work and coming home exhausted and spending my free time with Dell. I hardly had the motivation to get up in the morning, much less move to England.

Now I wish I had pulled myself out of that depression and come to live with Aunt B at Promise House. We could have run the bookshop together and I would have spent the last year with her. Maybe she wouldn't have died if I had been there with her. Or maybe she wouldn't have gone waking along the cliffs every night if I was here. Maybe she was just as lonely as I was and the nightly walks were something that kept her from going crazy within the walls of Promise House. I was over in Boston drowning in depression and my only living relative was here alone. We could have been good for each other.

Now it's too late.

She's gone and there's just me.

'How far back does the store go?' Dell asks, peering toward the back of the shop.

'There's more to the place than you can see. There's a turning at the back there which leads to more rooms and there's an upstairs too.'

'Oh my God, this place is huge!'

'Yeah, it's like a maze.'

'And now it's your maze.'

'That's what scares me. How am I supposed to control all this when I can barely control myself?'

'You'll be fine, Amy. Plus, you have me for a few more days to help get the place up and running.'

'I'm going to miss you, Dell.' I can feel tears welling up in my eyes and I see the same thing happening to Dell.

She sniffs and says, 'Hey, we have work to do.'

I nod but don't speak because if I do, my voice will crack and the tears will come and I'll be a useless mess and so will Dell.

The telephone on the counter rings suddenly, making us both jump. It's an old-fashioned phone with a dial and its ringtone isn't even a ringtone, it's actual bells inside the plastic casing of the phone.

Dell puts a hand on her chest as if to avoid a heart attack. 'Our first customer!' she says.

I pick up the handset and say, 'Promise Books, how may I help you?' in an exaggerated business voice. Dell cracks up and tries not to laugh out loud so I can hear the caller.

It's a young woman voice. 'Is this Miss Anderson?'

Technically I AM Miss Anderson, although probably not the one she's calling. 'Yes, this is she,' I say. Dell slides down onto her butt and sits on the floor laughing at my performance.

'It's the Meow Meow Cattery here, Miss Anderson. Just a courtesy call to remind you that Mr Tibbles is ready to be collected today.'

Mr Tibbles! I forgot about Aunt B's black cat. I never realized that he wasn't at the house. How could I forget Mr Tibbles? And what was he doing at a cattery? Had one of Aunt B's friends put him in there after the accident?

'I'll be along to collect him later today,' I tell the woman, 'but I don't have access to my address book at the moment. Could you remind me of your address, please?' There's a little metal pail of pens and pencils on the counter and a notepad next to the phone. I write down the address of the Meow Meow Cattery, thank the woman and hang up.

'What was that about?' Dell asks.

'Aunt B's cat, Mr Tibbles. I forgot all about him. He's in a cattery.'

'Cool, so let's go get him.'

I frown at the address on the notepaper. 'It's not going to be that simple. The cattery is in Penzance.'

She raises an eyebrow. 'That's miles away.'

'It's a half hour drive. I don't understand. How would Aunt B's cat end up so far away? There must be places closer to Promise Cove where he could have been taken. And who put him there in the first place? And why is today the day he was scheduled to come back out?'

Dell stands up and looks at me with mock seriousness. 'There's only question you need to ask yourself, Nancy Drew.'

'What's that?'

'"What time am I going to call Stoker?"'

'Dell, no.'

'You don't have a choice. You need to get the cat, right? And you need to drive there, right? Then you need Stoker.'

'There really are buses, you know.'

'You're going to take a cat on a bus?'

I sigh. I don't understand what's going on but Dell is right. I need to drive. I need Stoker. Maybe I'll find out more about who put Mr Tibbles in the cattery when I get there but I need to get there first and for that I need the car.

'What about the bookshop?'

'I'll stay here and give you and the hot mechanic some quality time. Leave it to me.' She sits on the swivel chair behind the counter and says, 'Now call him.'

'He's probably busy,' I say as I pull my phone out of my pocket. My hand is shaking as I lay the phone on the counter and dig back in my pocket for Stoker's card. Why the hell do I feel like a giddy girl calling a boy to ask for a date? He offered to teach me and I'm just taking him up on his offer. Nothing more.

I place the card on the counter and flip it over so his number is facing me. I punch the numbers into my phone and listen to the ringing. I want my hand to stop shaking. This is ridiculous. Luckily, Dell is busy playing with the cash register buttons and hasn't noticed.

He answers and says, 'Hello?'

He doesn't know my number so the caller ID on his phone won't have told him it's me and there's still time to hang up and find another way to get Mr Tibbles from Penzance.

'Hello?' he repeats.

'Stoker,' I say, clearing my throat, 'it's Amy here. Amy Anderson.' The confidence and playfulness I had when I was on the phone to the Meow Meow Cattery has fled.

'Hi,' he says. Does he sound pleased to hear from me? Wary? Was he just being polite when he gave me his number?

'I have a problem,' I say. No, don't tell him you have a

problem. Boys don't like girls with problems! Who cares? I only want him to teach me to drive a stick shift, nothing else.

'OK,' he says. Definitely wary.

'Well it's not really a problem. I just need to be somewhere today and I need to drive there.'

'Where?'

'Penzance.'

'Cool.'

No, not cool. I don't want to be doing this. I shouldn't be bothering him while he's at work. I can hear noises in the background. Hammering and something that sounds like welding. He has things to do that are way more important than helping me get to Penzance.

He says, 'How does half past two sound? I can get an hour off.'

'Two thirty? Yes, that sounds great.'

The noises in the background suddenly fade and it sounds like he's walked outside the garage so he can hear me better. But he speaks lower, as if he doesn't want the the other people in the garage to hear him. 'OK, I'll be at your house at two thirty and we'll take the Volvo. Don't worry, you'll pick it up in no time.'

'I'm actually at the bookshop. Could you possibly pick me up here then we can go get the car?'

'Sure, no problem.'

'OK, see you then,' I say and hang up. I exhale a long breath then notice Dell watching me. She's grinning.

'Woohoo. A date.'

'No, a driving lesson.'

She puts on her movie trailer voice. 'It began with a girl, a boy and a cat. It started as a driving lesson but became so much more.'

I throw the notepad at her but she dodges it, giggling.

'He'll be here in a few hours,' I say, 'so we have time to get things sorted here.'

'You're forgetting the most important thing.'

'What's that?'

'Flip the 'Closed' sign over. We are open for business.'

I turn the sign over so it displays 'OPEN' to the street and a man comes in immediately, as if he's been waiting out there for the store to open. He looks like he's in his mid to late twenties and he has a wide face and short-cropped far hair. His eyes are blue and piercing. He's wearing black shoes, formal pants and a dark trench coat over a white shirt and powder blue tie. 'Morning,' he says with a nod as he walks past us to the stack of detective novels near the back of the shop.

Dell looks at me with wide eyes and a grin that says. 'We got a customer!'

I hesitate, unsure what to do. Should I ask him if I can help him? Leave him to browse on his own? Maybe he doesn't want a pushy salesperson in his face. He seems to know what he's looking for as he takes paperbacks out of the racks, pages through them and replaces them. He chooses one and sets it aside while he looks for another. I'm rocking back and forth on my feet, desperate to keep my first customer happy but wary of scaring him off. Dell waits calmly behind the counter checking her black nail polish.

He comes back with three second-hand paperbacks. They're all pulpy crime books with lurid covers. He places them on the counter and pulls his wallet from the inside pocket of his trench coat.

'You're in luck, Sir,' Dell says, ringing up his purchases, 'because you are the first customer under our new management so you get three books for the price of two.' She offers him a smile.

'Sounds good,' he replies, thumbing bills out of his leather wallet. 'New management. So that means one of you two young ladies must be Amy Anderson.'

'That's me,' I say.

He hands the money to Dell and turns to face me while she finds a paper bag under the counter and slides his books into it.

'I'm sorry about your aunt,' he says with what sounds like genuine sympathy. Maybe he knew her. He could be a regular here who spent time talking to Aunt B every day. He could be her best friend for all I know, although I didn't see him at the funeral or at the house afterward.

'Thanks.'

Dell hands him his bagged books and his change. He takes them and says to me, 'It's a terrible shame that your aunt had her life cut short like that.'

'Yes,' I agree, 'it is.'

'When a woman who goes walking along those cliffs at night in all weathers suddenly falls on a clear rainless night, it's almost enough to make you wonder if there wasn't foul play involved.'

'Foul play? I'm sorry, who are you? Were you a friend of my aunt?'

He smiles and shakes his head. 'Not exactly. My name's Peter Macbeth. I'm a detective with the Penzance Police Force.' He shows me his ID.

'Detective? I don't understand.' Why is a police detective questioning me about Aunt B? Is he saying her death wasn't an accident? This doesn't make sense. Nobody mentioned the police being involved in an investigation.

'Miss Anderson, your Aunt's accident does seem on the surface to be just that…an accident…but we need to follow up on the cases like this. It's purely routine.'

'Cases like this?' I need to sit down. The bookshop is swirling in my vision and I'm afraid I'm going to faint. I reach out for the counter and steady myself.

'Do you need to sit down?' he asks with what sounds like genuine concern. Dell appears behind me and guides me to the swivel chair. I sit there taking deep breaths. Don't panic. Stay calm. Breathe.

Macbeth leans on the counter. 'I'm not suggesting that your aunt was the victim of foul play, I'm merely pointing out that some aspects of her accident seem to be worth investigating further. Your aunt was a young woman who had a lot of experience on those cliffs. I'm sure she herself would want us to look into every aspect of her death and leave no stone unturned.'

'So what has your investigation uncovered so far?' Dell asks.

'Nothing,' he replies. 'And that's good news. Nobody wants to think that your aunt's death was anything but an accident. But if you think of anything that may help us in our investigation, please contact me on this number.' He slides a business card across the counter. I don't look at it. I can't. What he has said…what he has suggested…that someone might have killed Aunt. B…I just can't take it in. There's no reason anyone would want to hurt my aunt. None.

'Anyway,' Detective Macbeth says a little uncomfortably, 'I'll keep in touch and let you know if we discover anything.' He leaves the store and the little bell rings to announce his departure.

'Are you OK?' Dell asks, stroking my head gently.

'I don't know. I had no idea Aunt B's death was being investigated as a murder.'

'That isn't what he said…'

'But it's what he meant.'

Murder. I can barely form the word in my mind. I feel like the world has suddenly changed and I have stumbled into a dark corner of it, a hidden place which contains secrets that may change my life.

'All we can do is wait and see if the police uncover anything,' Dell says. 'Like Macbeth said, it's just routine. They don't expect to find anything.'

I nod but I feel numb inside.

I don't know what to think anymore. The people beyond the bookshop window are all strangers to me, strangers living unknown lives. Could the sleepy town of Promise Cove be harboring my aunt's killer?

CHAPTER
FIVE

AMY

Stoker arrives at exactly two thirty and pulls up outside the store in a dark blue Land Rover which has a winch on the back. The words STOKER AUTOS are painted on the side in gold paint. Seeing him sitting out there waiting for me makes my heart skip a beat and I'm not sure why. I'm probably just nervous about having to make conversation with him all the way to Penzance and back. At least learning the gearshift will give us something to talk about. It isn't like this is a first date or anything.

'Your carriage awaits,' Dell says.

'Are you sure you'll be OK here on your own?'

'Do you see any customers? I'll be fine. Meet you at the house later. I'll be getting a taxi. No way am I walking back up those cliffs. What do you want for dinner tonight? I'll grab something from the market.'

'You decide.' I can't think about that right now, not while Stoker is waiting. And the bombshell that Detective Macbeth dropped on me earlier has my mind reeling.

'OK, you go and be swept off your feet by the handsome mechanic.' She pushes me out the door.

I stand on the sidewalk and Stoker looks up and sees me. He's wearing blue overalls open at the top to reveal a white t-shirt beneath. Seeing his ruggedly handsome face again sends tingles sparking through my body. Why does he have this effect on me? I don't like it. I like to control the situations I find myself in as best I can. Just a glance from Stoker makes me loose any semblance of control and sends my senses into overdrive. Not good.

When he sees me, the expression on his face turns to concern. He opens the passenger door and says, 'Amy, are you OK?'

I nod but don't say anything as I climb into the Land Rover. I don't trust myself to open my mouth right now. I don't know what I might say or if I'll be able to speak at all. Our first meeting was enough for him to classify me as 'probably crazy' and I don't want to do anything to turn that 'probably' into 'definitely'.

'Yeah, I'm fine.' I don't know if he's really interested in my emotional state or if he's just being polite. We hardly know each other so I'm guessing it's his English politeness that makes him seem concerned. But even so, how can he read my mood and guess that something is wrong? Am I that easily read? People can't usually read my moods at all so I'd be surprised if he can pick up on subtle shifts in my behavior since he doesn't really know me.

Yet.

His word. Meaning he wants to get to know me.

Yes, he wants to get to know me. Until he actually gets to know me. Then he'll want to run away from the crazy girl he once thought was worth getting to know.

At least for now he's interested in talking to me. So don't screw it up.

We drive along Main Street and he seems to be thinking of a way to break the ice. Finally he says, 'So how is the bookshop? Think you'll be OK there?'

'I love the shop. I can remember exploring it when I was younger. The sights and smells of that shop are part of my childhood. It feels like home.'

'And Promise House? I guess that's the same for you.'

I don't mention that everywhere I look in the house I imagine my mom and aunt growing up there. Instead I just nod and say, 'Yeah, I like it.'

We continue on in silence. I don't know what to say to him and this was a really bad idea. He probably already thinks I'm a dork and now I'm proving him right. This is a disaster. Think of something to ask him. Ask him anything. I go to open my mouth but he cuts me off before I can speak.

'So you said you have to go to Penzance? It's a long way for your first lesson in the car.'

'I have to go get my aunt's cat.'

'Mr Tibbles? What's he doing in Penzance?'

He knows the name of Aunt B's cat? Add that to the

fact that he knew Aunt B well enough to fix her car for free and I think there's more to Stoker's relationship with my aunt than he's telling. She always taught me to look for things that don't fit and this doesn't fit. Why would she have a close relationship with Stoker? She was thirty two and he's nineteen or twenty. She was into literature and the arts. I don't know much about Stoker…yet…but the only times I've seen him have been related to cars. He drives a Land Rover with a big winch on the back for God's sake. That doesn't mean he can't be into the arts, I guess, but he seems like a typical mechanic to me. He has grease on his face and neck right now and those cuts and grazes on his knuckles make me think that if there is something more to him, it's probably something I don't want to know about.

We pull into the driveway of Promise House and I let out a little breath of relief. At least from here on out I am going to be driving and he is going to be giving me instructions, which will give us something to say to each other. I feel weird because I'm physically attracted to him yet we have nothing at all in common.

Even the fact that I'm attracted to him weirds me out. This is the first time I've ever felt like this. The boys I dated back home all asked me out and I usually said yes because I really wanted people to like me and dating was a way to increase your social status, especially in school. I didn't really care much for the social status thing but I hated being on the bottom rung. So if a popular football player or a guy who was considered desirable asked me out, I always said yes. But even the desirable guys didn't seem desirable to me. Dell once asked me if I didn't like guys at all but I knew I was straight because all my dreams and fantasies about love and sex involved men. Never real men, not even pop stars or actors, but faceless men whose features I could never quite imagine clearly.

And now for the first time, I'm experiencing what all the girls were talking about and I understand what they meant when they described a boy as 'dreamy' or a 'hunk'. I feel those things about Stoker. I wish I didn't because it's making me act weird.

'Amy?' he says.

I realize he's parked on the driveway and cut the engine and opened his door already. And I've been sitting here daydreaming. Great.

'Sorry.' I open my door and climb out. 'I'll just get the keys.' I leave him on the driveway and I enter the house to get the garage and car keys from the rack by the door. Get a hold of yourself, Amy, and don't phase out. Try to keep a hold of reality or he really is going to think you're a mental case or something.

I go back out and hand him the keys. ''You want to get the car out of there and I'll take it from there?'

He nods and unlocks the garage then lifts the door. I wait by the Land Rover while he reverses the Volvo out of the garage and turns it around so it's facing the road.

'She's all yours,' he says, sliding from the driver's seat across to the passenger seat.

I get into the driver's seat and adjust the rearview and side mirrors and slide the seat forward so I can reach the pedals. Stoker watches me with some amusement on his face.

'What?'

'It's just that you look so serious.'

'Well this *is* serious. I want to get it right.'

'You will, don't worry. You can drive can't you?'

'Yes.'

'So all you need to learn is this little extra thing…the gears. You'll pick it up in no time.' He sounds more confident in me than I am in myself. That's kind of nice.

'OK. Do we need the GPS to find the way?'

'No, I know the way. Now, the car is in neutral at the moment. Put your hand on the gear shift and feel how it moves freely.'

I place my hand on the gear stick and wobble it around. 'OK, it moves.'

'Now you're going to put her into first. See the diagram on the top of the stick? It tells you where the gears are so first is slightly to the left and forward. To change gear, you need to press the clutch in. That's the pedal on the left. And anytime the car is in gear but you aren't pressing the accelerator…the gas…you need to put the clutch in or the car will stall.'

I bite my lip and nod. 'OK.'

'So put her in first.'

'Do you always refer to cars as 'her'?'

'Yes and you're playing for time so let's go. First gear.'

I depress the clutch and push the gear shift into first position.

'Now be careful when you let the clutch come back up because…'

I release the clutch too fast and the car jerks forward

twice before stalling. A red light on the dash shines at me accusingly.

'OK,' Stoker says, 'let's put our seat belts on before we go any further.'

We do that and I notice a grin on his face. 'You better not be laughing at me.'

'I'm not laughing at you.'

'So why are you grinning?'

'You get flustered easily. It's cute.'

Cute? I start the Volvo again and slam it into first gear, lifting the clutch until I feel it bite and the car starts to move forward toward the road.

'Now you've got it,' he says.

Cute? I give the car more gas and we go past the end of the driveway and onto the road. I have no idea where we're going so I take a right, away from town. The car is picking up speed but it's still in first gear and the engine is screaming.

'You need to change to second now,' Stoker advises.

Cute? I stomp on the clutch and pull the gear shift back hard into second. The gears crunch and the stick shakes in my hand. I let the clutch up too fast and the car kangaroos, throwing us about until it stalls again in the middle of the road.

'Let's try that again,' he says calmly.

'Cute? Really?' I start the car for a third time and push the stick into first gear, willing myself to do it right this time. I let up the clutch and we move forward slowly. The revs increase and the engine starts to whine.

'Time for second,' Stoker says, 'but this time pull the

stick back gently.' He puts his hand in mine and suddenly I can't concentrate on anything except the warm touch and comforting feeling of having his hand there. 'Put the clutch in,' he says calmly. How can he act so calmly while he's making me lose my mind?

I press my left foot on the clutch and Stoker pulls back smoothly on the gear shift, his hand feeling so good on mine. So right. I can't think about anything else and I take my foot off the clutch. The Volvo jack rabbits to a stop.

'When you're ready, start the car again.' He doesn't remove his hand from where it sits on top of mine.

I feel tears springing from my eyes and I can't believe I'm doing this, can't believe I'm going to break down in front of this boy who I hardly even know and he's going to see me crying. A sob escapes me and I wipe at my face with the hand he isn't touching.

'Hey, hey, it's OK, Amy. You're doing great.'

'It isn't that,' I say and I hate how my voice is cracking, 'it's the police. They came to the book store today and they said they're investigating…investigating…' I feel a sudden sadness rip through me and I start to sob uncontrollably.

Stoker takes his hand off mine and removes his seat belt then shifts in his seat so he' facing me. He puts his arm around me and pulls me toward him so my face is pressed against his chest. He smells of oil and gas with an underlying masculine scent. I grab his overalls in my fists and cry against him, feeling protected in his embrace . 'They think…she might…have been…murdered,' I sob. My eyes sting from the tears and I need to blow my nose. I hate that

I've broken down like this in front of him. What must he think of me?

He opens the glove box and finds a box of Kleenex. He pulls three out and passes them to me.

'Thanks.' I blow my nose as quietly as I can and wipe my eyes. Get a grip, Amy. This guy is really going to think you're psycho. I sit up again, already missing his strong arms around me but embarrassed that he felt the need to comfort me because I'm such a stupid mess. 'I'm sorry.'

'It's fine,' he says reassuringly. 'Did they really say that? Murder?'

'Not that actual word but he said foul play. And they have to investigate Aunt B's death because it was strange that she'd fall on a clear summer evening when she was used to walking around there in all seasons and weathers.'

He looks out through the windshield but I'm pretty sure he isn't looking at the road ahead. He seems lost in his thoughts. I guess if he knew my aunt as well as the evidence suggests - like how did he know there was a box of Kleenex in the glove compartment - then the fact that the police are investigating her death will be a shock to him as it was to me. I want to ask him how well he knew Aunt B but a part of me is actually afraid to hear the answer. I don't know why I'm being so ridiculous about this whole situation. If he was involved with my aunt, it really isn't any of my business. But if he was involved with her, why didn't he turn up to her funeral? Maybe I'm reading too much into this. The problem is I really do like him and that's getting in the way of just getting to know him.

I have no idea what he's thinking. He stares out of the car, his strong features unreadable.

'We should probably get going,' I say, 'we're in the middle of the road.'

'Err, yeah. Luckily this is a quiet road. OK, start the car when you're ready. Put her into neutral first.'

I do as he says. 'OK, she's in neutral.'

'Now put her into first.'

I press the clutch and gently move the stick into position. 'She's in first. I think she wants to move forward.'

He glances at me sideways with those perfect gray eyes. 'Are you mocking me?'

I look at him innocently. 'I'm sure I don't know what you mean.'

'Calling the car "she" like that.'

'I'm merely following your instructions. You're the instructor so if you say she's a she then she's definitely a she.'

He smiles. 'Right. Move her forward and remember to change gears gently.'

I let the clutch up and we move along the road.

Stoker puts his hand on mine again and I'm not sure whether it's to make sure I get the gear changes right or to comfort me after my breakdown or maybe even to comfort himself.

Either way, I like it.

I like it a lot.

————

Thirty minutes later, we're approaching Penzance on a road that runs by the sea. I have the shift down now and I haven't stalled the car or crunched the gears for at least ten minutes. In my mind I have a mantra that I keep repeating to myself, Push the clutch, change gear, let the clutch up slow. It's also ten minutes since Stoker took his hand from where it covered mine and I miss it like crazy.

'So where are we going to find the elusive Mr Tibbles?' he asks as we drive into the small town.

'At a place called Meow Meow.'

He nods. 'I think I know where that is. Park here in this car park.' He points to a parking lot on the left. I drive in and park the car and we get out. It's a warm summer day and to everyone else we probably look like a couple on a date. Except that Stoker is wearing overalls. And he's covered in grease. OK, we don't look like a couple on a date. At all. My fantasies are running ahead of reality again.

He heads for a cluster of stores and I catch up with him. 'Can I ask you something?'

'Of course.'

'Are there any places like catteries or kennels closer to Promise Cove?'

He thinks for a moment then says, 'Yeah, there are two that I can think of. Maybe more.'

'So how did Aunt B's cat end up way the hell out here?'

He shrugs. 'I have no idea. Why?'

'Doesn't it seem strange that someone would bring Mr Tibbles here? It's a half hour drive and there are at least two places closer to home.'

'I don't know, maybe Meow Meow serves the best cat food or something. Beth really does…did…love that cat.'

Again he lets slip the fact that he knew Aunt B and again I let it go unquestioned. None of my business.

'But that doesn't make sense either,' I tell him. 'Why would Aunt B put him in a cattery just before she died? How could she know that was going to happen?' Before I finish the last sentence a cold thought chills me and spreads up my spine like ice. Oh my God, what if Aunt B *did* know she was going to die?

What if she put her cat here so he would be fed and safe until I got here from America? But that that would mean she *jumped* from the cliffs. Could she really have calmly put Mr Tibbles in the Meow Meow knowing it was the last time she was gong to see him because of what she planned to do? And why would she even do that anyway? I can't believe Aunt B would commit suicide, I really can't. But it would explain a lot.

It would make sense of the fact that she fell from the cliffs despite the night being clear and dry. It would explain Mr Tibbles being in a cattery, but not why he is in one so far away from Promise Cove.

It would also let me understand, if only a little, why Mom did what she did a year ago. I know that depression can be genetic and suicide can run in families.

Does that mean I'm next? Maybe Aunt B was lonely living in Promise House all by herself with only her customers for company. And now that fate has befallen me. Am I going to go crazy in that house alone?

But was my aunt actually all alone in Promise House or

did she have Stoker there to keep her company? I look at him sideways only to realize he's looking at me with that concerned look on his face.

'What?' I ask.

'You kind of faded out there.'

'Sorry, I'm just trying to make sense of it all.'

'You think a lot.'

I shrug. 'And you don't? Do you just act without thinking?'

That may have hit a raw nerve because his eyes suddenly become sad and he says, 'Sometimes it's better to not think.'

Before this becomes a mutual depression-fest on the sidewalk, I say, 'OK, well you can think about where the Meow Meow Cattery is, right?'

The look passes from his face and he nods. 'It's just up this street.'

'So let's go.'

The Meow Meow is situated between a shoe shop and a dry cleaners. We go in and find ourselves in a small reception area. Behind the desk, a girl with thick-rimmed glasses and red hair tied back into a pony tail is typing into a computer. From behind a door at the back of her office, I can hear faint meowing coming from some of the residents.

She looks up, sees Stoker, and unconsciously smooths down her skirt. 'Hello, can I help you?'

'I'm here to pick up my cat,' I say to get her attention away from Stoker.

'What name is it please?'

'Anderson.'

'Your cat's name is Anderson?'

'No, *my* name is Anderson. My cat's name is Mr Tibbles.'

'Mr Tibbles,' she repeats, typing into the computer. 'Ah, yes, I spoke to you on the phone this morning.'

'That's right.'

'You sounded a bit different then.'

I remember the fake voice I put on earlier and nod.

'Well Mr Tibbles' bill is paid in full so I'll just go and get him for you.' She a few more keystrokes and nods. 'Yes, we have you cat carrier here from when you brought him in.' She gets up and goes through the door at the back. 'Back in a moment,' she shoots at Stoker over her shoulder with a smile.

I look over at him and he just shrugs.

'Does this happen everywhere you go?'

'Not everywhere, no.'

'Really? Girls don't just throw themselves at you everywhere? I am surprised.'

'You didn't,' he says.

That throws me off guard and I don't know how to reply. 'Well…no…' I stammer, 'I don't really…throw myself at guys.'

'I see.'

'No, you don't. I mean, I like guys. I just don't throw

myself at them so even if I liked you, I wouldn't be throwing myself at you.' Way to ramble on, Amy.

'If?'

I nod, giving nothing away. 'Yes…if.'

'I suppose 'if' is something for me to work with.'

When he says that, I feel a sudden surge of endorphins in my body like I'm on a high from running a race and I'm sure my pupils are dilating. My pulse is hammering and I feel very warm. I lean on the reception counter and try to speak calmly. 'What…what is that supposed to mean?'

'Just what I said. I like you, Amy.'

'OK.' Say something more. Don't clam up now! My mind scatters around trying to find a response but I don't have anything else to say. I feel like my legs might give way they're shaking so bad.

The redhead returns with a cat carrier. She places it on the counter and inside I can see Mr Tibbles jet black fur and emerald green eyes. 'Hello, Mr Tibbles,' I say looking in at him.

He lets out a pitiful meow.

'He's ready to go home,' the redhead says. 'I'll just find the form you signed when you brought him in and get you to sign it to say that you've collected Mr Tibbles.' She opens a filing cabinet and flicks through the papers inside.

Another cry comes from the cat carrier and the redhead speaks in a voice like she's speaking to a two year old, 'Oh he's been a good boy and now he's ready to go home.'

Mr Tibbles goes silent.

She comes back with a piece of paper. The printed form has been filled out with the address of Promise House, Mr

Tibbles' name and at the bottom is a signature that makes me catch my breath. Clearly written in black pen in the box that is marked "Owner's Signature" are the words 'Beth Anderson' in my aunt's handwriting. So she did bring the cat here herself before she died.

With a shaky hand, I sign the box that says "Animal Collected By" and slide the form back across to the receptionist. She places it back into the cabinet and says, 'Is there anything else I can help you with?' The question is clearly directed at Stoker.

'No, we're good,' I say and head for the door holding the handle of the cat carrier.

'Here, let me take that,' Stoker says as we get out onto the sidewalk. He takes Mr Tibbles off me and we walk back to the car.

A part of me wants him to continue the conversation we were having before the stupid receptionist came back but he seems to have forgotten it or is purposely not mentioning it. Instead, he says, 'I bet Mr Tibbles will be glad to get back to Promise House.'

'Did you see the signature on that form?' I ask him, 'it was Aunt B. She brought him here. Why? I don't understand.'

'Maybe we'll never know.'

'No, there has to be a reason. Aunt B used to be always reading detective novels and she would tell me that if something seems out of place, there's a reason. She made up treasure hunts for me when I was a kid and had me hunting all over Promise House for trinkets or candy prizes she had hidden. The clues she left me were always things out of their normal place or somewhere they didn't belong.'

'You think your aunt is leaving you clues? To what?'

'No, I don't mean that. It's just that Mr Tibbles being in Penzance is something that's out of place.'

'But we don't know what it means.'

'No, we don't.'

'So we'll probably never know now. We should just take him home and forget all about it. At least he's OK.'

We reach the car and Stoker says, 'I'll drive back if you like. You've had a good practice with the gears today.'

'Thanks, that's kind of you.' I put Mr Tibbles on the back seat and slide into the passenger side. Stoker gets in and starts the car and we pull out of the parking lot. It's a relief to not have to drive all the way back to Promise Cove.

My phone rings and I pull it out of my jeans. It's Dell.

'Hey, I sold some books!' she says as I answer.

'Great. Did we have many customers?'

'After that detective guy there were a few couples who were on vacation and wanted beach books and a family that wanted books for their kids. I've closed up now and I'm waiting for the taxi to come pick me up. How's it going with the hunky mechanic? Have you been handling the stick?'

I want to tell her to stop being crude but if I did, Stoker would wonder what we were talking about.

'Yes, it went well.'

'Ooh, that good, huh? When are you seeing him again?'

'You have the spare key to get into the house if you're

back before me,' I say calmly, 'so I'll see you later. We're on our way back.'

A long sad meow comes from the back seat.

'The cat doesn't sound too happy,' Dell says.

'Would you be happy if you were stuck in a plastic carrier?'

'I guess not. But I'd be happy if I was stuck in a car with Dean Stoker.'

'See you soon, Dell.'

'Cool. Ooh, we have fish for dinner. Will Stoker be joining us?'

'No.'

'Okies. See you in a bit.'

I hang up and shake my head at Dell's persistence.

'Everything good?' Stoker asks.

'Yes. Everything's good.'

———

Stoker

I like her. I really like her. There's something about her that makes me want to know more, to learn all I can about what she likes and doesn't like and what her life in America was like and what she thinks to living here. There's also a sadness around her. It sits on her shoulders like a dark cloak and in those times when she spaces out, I know she's thinking of the things that make her sad. I want to hold her tight and tell her it's all going to be alright but I don't even know what's wrong.

Just like I don't know her very well, she doesn't know me either…not the real me. She probably just sees the oily mechanic and nothing else. I can't blame her for that, I've hardly been forthcoming about myself. I even told her I don't think much, which isn't true.

I went too far in the Meow Meow when I said I her 'if' was something I could work on. What was I thinking? That's the sort of thing a jackass says. Thank God the receptionist came back just in time.

Sometimes Amy seems like a frightened rabbit and I feel that if I move too fast she's going to bolt and I'll never see her again.

I don't want that.

I want to see her again soon but I'm not even sure she would have called me if she hadn't been stuck for a way to get to Penzance. Before we get back to Promise House, I'll ask her out. There are loads of things to do around the cove and she probably doesn't know half of them.

If she wants to wait until her friend Dell goes back to America, that's fine. I'm sure they want to spend this week together. I can wait to see her but I can't wait to ask her. Then we'll have a definite date to get together. I'll have more time to plan it out then, make sure she enjoys herself.

We're about three minutes from Promise House. I have to do it now. If Dell is waiting on the drive when we get to the house, I won't be able to ask.

Now.

It's got to be now.

'Amy.'

She looks over at me. She was daydreaming again, probably about the riddle of the cat. I have no idea why Beth would put Mr Tibbles in a cattery in Penzance but I'm sure there's a rational explanation behind it.

'I was wondering if you'd like me to show you around Promise Cove sometime.' There. Said it. It's out.

She frowns. 'I know my way around Promise Cove. I've been here a few times.'

'Really? Do you know the sea caves on the cliff face? The hidden beaches along the coastal path? There's a new coffee shop in town, you know. I bet that wasn't here the last time you came.' Doesn't she realize I'm asking her out? I wasn't clear enough. I've blown it. And now we're at her house. Shit.

I park on the drive and get ready to make myself clearer when the front door opens and Dell comes out of the house. I sigh. Not to worry there's plenty of time. I've got Amy's number on my phone from when she rang me. Don't panic, just play it cool.

Amy grabs the cat carrier and I get out of the car. 'You want me to put it in the garage for you?'

'No, it's OK. It's a nice evening so I think it'll survive out here until morning. Sorry…*she'll* survive.' She flashes me a smile that makes me feel a tightness in the pit of my stomach. I have got get to know this girl better.

'Thanks for the driving lesson and everything,' she adds.

'No problem. If you need me again, you've got my number.'

Dell comes over. 'Yes she has and she will use it, don't you worry.'

'OK, well I guess I should get back to work.' I told Dad I was taking a late lunch hour because I was busy working on Mrs Frank's Fiesta and I didn't want to stop for lunch until I'd replaced her brake cable. I don't know if he believed me or not. He doesn't trust me anymore.

I climb into the Land Rover and wave to the girls. They're both standing on the drive waiting to wave me off with Mr Tibbles' carrier on the ground between them.

I roll down my window. 'You might as well let him out. He has a cat flap in the back door so he can come and go as he pleases anyway and he spends a lot of time outdoors. There's no way he's going to get lost anywhere within ten miles of this place.'

Amy nods and opens the little plastic gate on the carrier. Mr Tibbles shoots out like a black rocket and scampers around the back of the house.

'I think he likes his freedom,' I say. 'See you later.'

I drive onto the road and take a left into town and the girls are still waving to me as I disappear from their sight behind the roadside hedge.

———

Dad is leaning under the bonnet of a Ford Focus in the garage car park when I get back. He looks over at me as I get out of the Land Rover then goes back to studying the Focus' engine. Just walk past him into the garage. Don't say anything. Just go inside and do the oil change on the Nova in there.

I walk past the Focus and almost make it inside the garage.

'Where have you been?'

'Late lunch. I told you.' I get my gloves from the workbench and put them on.

'Yeah, but where?'

'I took a drive. Didn't feel like eating.'

'Drive to where?'

'Does it matter?'

He comes out from beneath the bonnet and stands square on to me. Standing there in the sun with his arms by his sides with a wrench gripped in his left hand he looks like an old gunfighter from a Western movie. Last of a dying breed.

'It matters,' he says.

Do I lie to him? I could lie to him but I don't want to and I don't see why I should have to. After all, I'm twenty years old and I can do as I damn well please. But if I tell him the truth it will hurt him. He'll drink even heavier tonight and we'll descend down into that hellish spiral again.

'I was out with a friend.'

'And this "friend" wouldn't happen to be Beth Anderson's niece would it?'

'I can see who I want, Dad.'

He comes two steps closer. 'Is she filling your head with the same stupid ideas her aunt was feeding you?'

I don't even answer that.

He shakes his head as if he's disgusted with me. 'Get in there and change the oil on that Nova. And don't get ideas above your station. James was too good for this place but don't start thinking you are. James could have made something of his life, could have been someone. But you… you're no one.' He returns to the Focus and shoves his head back under the bonnet.

I get into the pit beneath the Nova and put an oil pan on the floor before using a torque wrench to take off the bleed screw. I watch as dark brown oil pours from the car and pools in the drip pan like old blood.

CHAPTER
SIX

GONE

AMY

I wake up fast, not knowing what I was dreaming about but knowing that I don't want to go back to sleep. I check my phone. Seven a.m. I groan and rest my head back on the pillow even though I don't close my eyes. I suddenly remember what day it is and feel a wave of depression threaten to drown me.

Today is the day Dell flies back to America.

I feel like crying but I have to put on a brave face for Dell. She already hates leaving me here and I don't want to make it any harder for her. She's been amazing the past six days, helping to get the bookshop back in business and doing most of the cooking around the house. Not to mention keeping me sane with her banter and making me laugh as she rates every male customer we get in the shop. And her constant ribbing about Stoker doesn't even bother me.

I haven't seen him for three days and the last time I saw him was in town. He looked like he was in a hurry, striding purposefully down Main Street, so I didn't catch his attention. I've been driving to town and back in the Volvo every day because Dell refuses to walk and now I'm pretty skilled with the gears but a part of me still wants to see more of Stoker.

I'm going to make Dell breakfast today. We have eggs, bacon, sausages and toast and I intend to make her a going away feast before the taxi comes to collect her at eleven thirty. Even though today is Friday and probably a good day for business, the bookshop is going to stay closed and I'm going to spend the last few hours with Dell doing whatever she wants to do, which means we'll probably just stay in the house and watch TV. Which is fine by me but before Dell gets up, there's something I need to do…something I've been meaning to do since I got a handle on how to drive the Volvo.

I leave my room and creep past Dell's door, even though a stampede of buffalo in the hallway wouldn't wake her. Her alarm is set for nine and until them she will be dead to the world.

I go down to the hallway and put my sneakers on and grab my brown leather jacket from the closet under the stairs. Then I go out through the kitchen to the back door. There's no sign of Mr Tibbles so I assume he's outside even though he usually spends the mornings in the kitchen meowing until he gets fed. I go out back and hug myself against the morning breeze. It looks like it will be a hot day but there is still some of the night chill in the air.

The sea pounds the the cliffs and the rhythmic sound of tons of water crashing against immoveable rock is somehow comforting. No wonder Aunt B loved it here.

But if she loved it so much here, why would she end it?

I've been thinking about this for days and the only explanation I can come up with is that she either took her own life or knew her life was in danger. The second theory sounds ridiculous, like something out of one of her detective novels. If she thought someone was going to kill her, she would have gone to the police.

So that can only mean suicide.

Mom and Aunt Beth.

Leaving just me.

Alone.

I shake that thought because it leads down some paths in my mind I don't want to journey along. Instead, I do what I came out here to do and pick some of the flowers in the garden beneath the kitchen window. When I have enough for two bouquets, I head back into the kitchen and lay then out on the table, selecting colors that look good together and arranging everything until I'm satisfied enough to tie them together with string and tie a white ribbon around each bouquet.

Then I go out front and lay them carefully on the back seat of the Volvo and drive out to the Sea Road Cemetery.

———

When I get to the cemetery, I have the biggest shock of the morning. Stoker's Land Rover is parked by the gate. It's definitely the one he gave me a ride in the other day; dark blue with STOKER AUTOS painted on the sides and the winch on the rear. What is he doing here? And at this time of the morning? 'Well obviously the same as you,' I tell myself. 'This is the only cemetery in town and I'm sure he knows people who have died.'

Wait a minute. What if he is here for *exactly* the same reason as me? What if he's visiting Aunt B's grave?

That would be just too weird.

Maybe I should come back later. No, there is no later… Dell leaves today and I have to cook breakfast and spend time with her.

I check myself in the rearview and groan. I didn't put on any makeup and my hair is a mess. I didn't think there would be anyone here so early. And I certainly didn't expect to meet Stoker. I don't have a choice. I want to put these flowers on the graves for Mom and Aunt B and if that means Stoker seeing my 'early morning' look then so be it. I'm sure he'll get over it.

I drive in through the gates and up the driveway that leads to the small parking lot, looking for Stoker among the rows of gravestones. I don't see anyone at all but the cemetery is planted with threes here and there so he could be out of my line of sight. I can see Aunt B's and Mom's graves from where I park the car and Stoker isn't there so maybe he's visiting someone else.

Taking the flowers, I lock the car and walk along the same pathway I walked a year ago when Mom was buried here and again last week when Aunt B was buried next to her. They had such short lives, hardly any time on the earth at all, and now they're going to be here at the Sea Road Cemetery...at the end of this little stone path... forever. At least they're together.

A noise behind me makes me turn around and there is Stoker in a black leather jacket and blue jeans walking toward the parking lot, head down with his hands in his pockets. He's so upset he walks right past my car without even seeing it. I don't call him. He looks like he wants to be left alone. Curious, I walk back along the path to the point where I think Stoker must have walked onto it from the rows of graves. I step onto the grass and behind a little stand of birch trees, I see the graves he was visiting. Two gravestones next to each other, each with a fresh bouquet of flowers placed in front of it.

Claire Stoker, beloved wife and mother. Always in our thoughts.

James Stoker, son of Claire and Max and brother of Dean. A life cut short. Gone but never forgotten.

The dates on the stones put their deaths on the same day fifteen months ago. James was only twenty one.

His mother and brother. There must have been some sort of accident.

Maybe Stoker and I do have something in common; we've both lost people we love.

And we both bring flowers to their graves.

I step back onto the path and walk to where my loved ones are buried. There are lots of flowers around Aunt B's headstone from the funeral and from her friends in

Promise Cove. I add mine and place the other bouquet on Mom's grave. I sit on the grass between them and feel a sudden overwhelming need to cry. I don't hold it back. I let it come and and soon the tears are stinging my face and I can't catch my breath because I'm crying so hard.

I don't want to be without them. Everything I do in my life will always feel a little duller because they won't be here to see it, to talk to me, to advise me or to laugh with me. I already feel numb inside most of the time and I'm the one who is still alive and should be experiencing life to the full. I feel like my soul is already dead and buried. The only time I feel anything is when I cut myself and I know that isn't how it's supposed to be and I have to stop doing it, I know that but it's so hard to give up the only thing that allows you to feel alive if only for a moment. Please help me stop. Please help me be normal.

———

By the time I get back to Promise House, Mr Tibbles is in the kitchen waiting to be fed but Dell is still asleep. She still has ten minutes before her alarm sounds.

Mr Tibbles winds himself around my legs as I get a can of cat food and open it. He meows as if he's telling me to hurry. I get it into his dish and he wolfs it down as soon as I put the dish on the floor. I give him a scratch behind his ears and set about making breakfast for Dell and me.

She finally makes an appearance as I'm getting every-thing out of the grill and frying pans.

'Something smells amazing,' she says.

'It's a special breakfast for a special person.'

'Oh boy, don't start going all soppy on my now. We have a couple of hours yet.'

'I know. It's just that I'm going to miss you like hell.'

'Me too. But at least we have Skype and Hangouts. It'll be just like I'm here in the room with you. And you have to keep me updated on the Stoker situation.'

'There is no Stoker situation.'

She picks up a piece of toast and takes a bite. 'I saw the way he looked at you after you guys came back from Penzance. Believe me, there's a Stoker situation.'

I shake my head. 'Nope. Haven't heard from him in a while now.'

She sits down at the table while I dish up the food. The kitchen is full of the smell of sausages and bacon and it smells somehow comforting. After today, I will be having oatmeal for breakfast before going to work in the shop alone and then returning to a TV dinner.

Mr Tibbles looks up at me with his green eyes and lets out a pitiful cry that is supposed to make me feel sorry for him and give him some real meat. It works and I put a sausage on his dish. He takes a bite and shakes his head because it's too hot. Undeterred, he grabs the sausage and takes it out through the cat flap.

'I've been thinking about why Stoker hasn't contacted you yet.'

'OK, let's hear this great theory.'

'Not so much theory as deduction.'

'Give it to me.'

'He's waiting until I leave. He knows I'm only here for

a week and he doesn't want to get in the way. So he's keeping his distance. After today, he'll be in touch.'

'If you say so.' I take our plates to the table and we start on the cooked breakfast.

'I do say so. Aww, that's really nice of him to resist his urges until I leave.'

'Urges?'

'Urges. Do we need to have 'the talk'? Hmm?'

'There's nothing like that going to happen. You know my experience with boys and how it all goes horribly wrong.'

'That's just because you didn't meet the right one yet. He could be the one.'

'Wow, you have a real talent at exaggerating reality.'

'I have a talent at seeing what is right in front of my eyes, something you should try sometime.'

'You're crazy, Dell.'

'I'm not crazy. Everyone else is crazy and I'm the only sane person in the world.'

'So what do you want to do this morning?'

"We're not opening the bookshop?'

'No, I want to spend the time with you.'

'Cool. Let's bum around and watch TV.'

I smile.

'What you smiling at?'

'You're not the only one who can predict things.'

'Hey, predicting that I would want to stay indoors and watch TV hardly makes you the Amazing Kreskin.'

'I know but it's nice to know that some things never change.'

'And what are you going to do this afternoon when I'm on my way to the airport? You could open the store then to keep yourself busy.'

'Nah, I'm probably going to watch old movies and eat ice cream.'

'Ice cream. I approve. But tomorrow when you open the book store, make sure you look your best. Wear something nice and not just this black shit you wear all the time.'

'That's rich coming from you.'

'Take my advice. You want to look good for him, don't you?'

'Who?' I ask innocently, knowing who she means and hoping deep down that she's right. Dell is good at reading people. She'd make a hell of a poker player if she could be bothered to learn the game.

'Him. The one. He's going to make his move tomorrow. Be prepared.'

'Do not start calling him 'the one'.'

'I'll call him whatever I damn well please, Missy. Anyway, who was I referring to?'

'Stoker.'

'Aha, so you admit Stoker is the one!'

We both break down into fits of giggles and all the time I'm aware of the clock ticking toward the eleventh hour when my best friend in the whole world will be gone.

―――――

The time passes way too fast. It isn't fair. We stand in the hallway by the front door, her suitcase packed in the typical Dell way of just throwing all her clothes inside and forcing the case shut. The taxi will be here any moment and then she'll be on her way home. According to the way things are now, *my* home is Promise House. It doesn't feel like home but neither does Boston anymore. I don't feel like I have a home anywhere at all.

'Safe journey, Dell.'

'That's the fifth time you've said that. I'll be fine. I'll text you when I get to the airport and when I land on the other side.'

'OK.' I try to hold back the threatening tears by swallowing hard.

'Hey, we'll get online tomorrow and have a good chat.' She has tears welling in her own eyes.

'I don't want you to go, Dell.'

She puts her arms around me and we hug. She starts to cry. 'I'm going to miss you,' she whispers.

'Me too.' I let the tears come and we stand there crying together until the taxi sounds its horn on the driveway.

'My ride is here,' she says, dabbing at her eyes with a Kleenex.

'Yeah. Make sure you text me.'

'I will.' She opens the door and goes out to the cab. The driver puts her case in the trunk and she gets into the back of the car, waving at me through the window as the taxi pulls away from the house and turns onto the main road. I stand at the open front door after she's gone and cry some more. I can't believe she's gone. A few hours ago we were having breakfast and laughing and now she isn't here anymore and the house is quiet. She won't be here for breakfast tomorrow. Or the next day. Or the day after that.

I return to the silent house and close the door.

I'm not going out today.

I feel too sad and tired.

I go into the living room and curl up on the sofa. When I was a little girl I used to lie here and watch the flames crackle and spark in the big stone fireplace. We had a fire in there last night while we sat watching TV and drinking soda and talking about nothing in particular.

Now the fire is dead and the fireplace is just a black square.

I close my eyes and let the tears roll hotly over my face.

My only friend.

Gone.

PART TWO
SECRETS

CHAPTER
SEVEN

AMY

I get out of bed the next morning to find Mr Tibbles in the kitchen waiting for his breakfast. The kitchen clock tells me it's only six o clock but I can't go back to sleep because I feel too restless. I already know that today is going to be a bad day and last night, the only thing that prevented me from using the razors in my nightstand was that I was just too tired. I fell asleep on the sofa after Dell left then wearily climbed the stairs a few hours later and collapsed on the bed. Now I'm paying for all that sleep with a restlessness that makes me feel like it's mid-morning, not six a.m.

It isn't even light out yet. There's a slight gray tinge to the sky but the sun isn't up. So why am I? I need to sort out my sleep patterns or I'll end up napping in the book-shop when I should be working.

I turn from the kitchen window and feed the cat then stand there for a moment listening to the silence of Promise House. It's way too early to open the shop but I need to get out from inside these four walls for a while. Maybe a walk along the cliffs will clear out the cobwebs in my head. It looks like a nice day out there. If I leave now, I can catch the sunrise.

Before I leave, I apply a little makeup and brush my hair, remembering my chance encounter with Stoker at the cemetery. I'll come back and change before I go into town so my blue jeans and short-sleeved blue sweater will be fine for the walk. The sleeves of the sweater are short but not too short; they come down to my elbows. I never have my upper arms exposed. Never. If I ever want the world to see how ugly I am inside, I just need to go out with bare arms. The scars tell the whole story.

I leave by the back door and the salty sea breeze feels good on my face. The tide is out and the stretch of sand beneath the cliffs is exposed and I consider taking a walk along the beach but I don't know anything about sea tides and if the waves come in while I'm down there and I can't find a way back up the cliffs, I'll be stuck. So I stick to the cliff tops and walk aimlessly along, waiting for the sun. The little dirt path I'm following has been created over the years by thousands of pairs of walking boots and is at least fifteen feet away from the edge of the cliffs and my mind runs over the possibility of Aunt B falling accidentally. I can't imagine it could happen that way. She knew the path and she walked it every night. No way could she fall over the edge. Even if she stumbled on a rock or something and fell towards the edge there's no way she would reach it; she'd just land on the grass.

The more I think about it, there's only one explanation. Aunt Beth jumped.

I walk carefully to the edge and look down. It's a long way. Further along the beach there's a man walking a dog, throwing a stick for it into the sea. The dog goes splashing in and grabs the stick and return to his owner shaking himself dry.

The stretch of sand ends where the rocky cliff juts out into the sea and there's another person down there, sitting by the rocks in front of what looks like a painter's easel. The tide must be out for a while if he has time to paint the landscape. I step back from the edge and continue along looking for one of the paths that wind down the cliff face to the beach. Maybe I can take a look at the painting and chat with the artist. I've heard that artists come to Cornwall for the quality of the light and that light is about to begin for the day as the sun comes up.

I find a trail that leads down to the beach and I take it, clambering over rocks and making sure I'm safe before taking each step down. It's steep but as long as I go slow I can make it. The climb back up is going to be a nightmare though. Maybe I'll be able to find an easier way back.

I let out a sigh of relief when I reach the beach and I trek over the sand toward the rocks where the painter is set up. He looks up and sees me and waves me over and I can't believe my eyes. It's Stoker. Dean Stoker the mechanic sitting on a beach at dawn painting the landscape. I walk a little faster, which is hard in the sand, and by the time I get to him, I'm exhausted.

He's sitting on a little fold-up stool and he has a small wooden easel onto which he's attached a watercolor pad. There's a palette of watercolor paints clipped onto the easel and an assortment of brushes sitting in a tray. A jar of water sits in the sand by Stoker's boots. He isn't his usual greasy self this morning; he's wearing a dark blue long-sleeved t-shirt with a rock band's logo across the chest and blue jeans with a black belt and black boots. He looks good. Really good.

'Hey, I didn't expect you to be up so early,' he says.

'I could say the same thing about you.'

'If you're going to paint a seascape at dawn, you need to be here at dawn. Take a seat. The sand's comfy.'

I sit on the sand and run my fingers through the tiny grains, making nonsense patterns.

'I didn't know you were a painter.'

'You didn't ask.'

'Stoker, don't be ridiculous. Why would I ask that?'

'You didn't ask because all you saw was the dirty mechanic in his overalls. And you thought that was who I am. All I am.'

I shrug. He isn't wrong on that score. I *did* think that but only because that was the one and only side of him that I saw.

'Have you been painting long?'

'Since I was a kid. Painting and drawing. It lets me

escape the world for a little while and concentrate on something that isn't depressing.'

'How do you mean?'

'Oh, you know…just life.'

I think about the graves of his mother and brother in the Sea Road Cemetery and nod. 'Yeah.'

He grab a brush and dips it into the water then the blue paint and he lays down a wash on the paper to represent the sky. 'So why are *you* up so early?'

'I couldn't sleep. Dell went home yesterday and I sorta fell asleep all afternoon and all night so I'm up bright and early today.'

'Well it's nice to see you.' He puts down a gray shape on the paper where the cliffs are.

'What are you painting?'

'You see that cliff there? The way it curves out into the sea? And just beyond it you can see a rock formation in the water. I want to capture that.'

I look around at the rocks above us and ask a question I hardly dare ask but which is burning inside me. 'Stoker, it it around here that…Aunt B…fell?'

He pauses and takes his brush from the paper. 'Yes. Just a little way back toward Promise House.'

Oh my God. So I actually walked past the spot Aunt B was standing when she fell. I look along the line of sand that runs beneath the cliffs. 'So…it's this beach…'

'Where they found her? Yeah, it is. A little further up that way. Some people put wreaths there but the tide took them.'

I try to imagine the spot where my aunt fell then I glance up at the cliff top where I was walking moments ago. The path up there is totally safe. There's no danger of falling over the edge. Is that why the police are investigating? Because they think she was thrown over the cliff edge? But they don't know that she put her cat in the cattery two days before she died. Even during her last days, she was thinking of the well-being of Mr Tibbles. She even went so far as to pay the bill so I wouldn't have to when I collected him. Everything tied up neatly. Then she jumped.

I don't know why. I'll probably never know why.

'Hey, Amy.'

Stoker is looking at me, his painting barely touched. 'You want to go for a coffee?'

'But your painting isn't finished.'

'I'd rather go for a coffee with you than sit here painting. Those cliffs aren't going anywhere. There's a beach front coffee shop in town called Sarah's Coffee And Cakes. They open early and they do a really nice coffee and…'

'No need to say any more, you had me at "cakes". I'd love to go.'

'Really? Cakes at this hour?'

'It's never too early for cake.'

He laughs and starts to pack away his painting equipment.

'You need any help?'

'No, I've got it. Everything folds down and fits in this little bag.' He holds up a black nylon bag. 'I travel light, especially when I'm painting because I sometimes have to sneak out of the house. I couldn't do that with a full-sized easel and canvasses.'

'Why do you have to sneak out?'

'My dad doesn't like me painting. Or drawing. Or even reading.'

'Why?'

'It's a long story.' He folds the easel up and stows everything away in the bag, which he slings over his shoulder. Seeing him in the tight t-shirt, I realize how muscular he is. He must go to the gym regularly to get a body like that. I stop my mind from going down that route; we were having a nice relaxed conversation and if I start thinking about this other stuff, I'll have trouble forming sentences.

'Let's go,' he says, 'your cake awaits.' He sets off toward the trail that leads up the cliffs.

'Did you walk here from home?' I ask him.

'No, there's a little parking area off the road up there. I came in the Land Rover.'

'Great.' I don't know if I can make it back up the trail and all the way into town, no matter how much cake is waiting at the finish line.

He starts to ascend and even though he has the bag on his shoulder, he's a lot faster than me and soon I'm puffing and panting and way behind him. He stops half way up and waits. As I catch up with him he reaches out his hand. I take it and we walk up hand in hand. It's nice. Really nice. I almost don't want to get to the top because I don't want him to stop holding my hand.

I've held hands with a few boys before but it was just

awkward. I didn't know what to do. Should I move my fingers a little? Stroke the back of their hand? It just seemed pointless. But with Stoker it feels natural, it feels right. I'm not even worrying about what to do with my hand or fingers because I don't feel like I *have* to worry about it.

He guides me to the top and we stand there for a moment still holding hands. The breeze feels so good up here and I close my eyes as it cools my face. Stoker stands close to me, still holding my hand.

'You OK?' he asks.

'Yeah, that feels so good.'

'The sea breeze?'

'Mm hmm.'

'I thought maybe you meant the fact that we're holding hands.'

'That feels good too,' I admit. Did I really just say that? Wait until Dell hears about it, she'll be giving me her best 'told you so' look and screaming down her webcam at me that she knew it all along. I'm sure I can handle her gloating because for the first time in my life, I actually feel something for a boy. I feel something when I look at him, when I touch him and even when I think about him.

'We should go before they run out of cake,' he says.

I open my eyes and smile at him. 'I thought you said only crazy people eat cake at this early hour.'

'I never said that.'

'You kind of implied it.'

We walk past the path to a cement area next to the road, still holding hands. Stoker's Land Rover is parked there. There are picnic tables on the grass here and a steel trash can on a wooden post. 'It's kind of a picnic area,' he says, 'for the tourists mainly.'

'Is that how you think of me, as a tourist?'

'Hell no. You were born here. You're a Cover through and through.'

'Cover? Did you just make that up?'

'Maybe. OK, how about Covian? Cove-Dweller?'

'And you call me crazy.'

'I told you, I never said that.'

'You implied it.'

'You want to drive' he asks, 'now that you're proficient with the gears?'

'How do you know I'm proficient?'

'I may have seen you driving the Volvo a couple of times around town.'

'Are you stalking me?'

He flashes me an innocent look. 'Me a stalker? Do I look like a stalker?'

'I don't know what a stalker looks like.'

'They look like mechanics mainly. Mechanics who paint.'

I laugh and get into the passenger side. 'You can drive. I don't want to drive this monstrosity.'

'Yes, ma'am.' He gets into his seat and reverses onto the road before heading toward town.

I look out of my window and smile. The sun has come up and has lit up the sea and the cove and the cliffs.

It's going to be a great day.

REVEAL

AMY

We get to Sarah's Coffee And Cakes and Stoker parks the Land Rover. I slide out and he takes my hand like it's the most natural thing in the world. And it feels like it is. We walk into the coffee shop together and a blonde lady in her forties behind the counter smiles at us. There are five other customers in here, even though it's still really early. Two businessmen in suits reading newspapers and drinking coffee and a couple in their twenties who look like they've been camping on the beach. They're eating pancakes. And an hispanic man who is wearing a suit and typing figures into a spreadsheet on his Macbook.

'Hey, Stoker,' the woman says, 'who's your friend?'

'Hi, Sarah. This is Amy. Amy Anderson. Amy…Sarah.'

I smile and say hello.

'Anderson? Are you Beth Anderson's niece from America?'

'Yes, that's right.' I seem to be semi-famous in Promise Cove.

'It's a real shame what happened to your aunt. She was a lovely young woman. Now what can I get you two?'

'Two coffees,' Stoker says, 'and I believe Amy wants some cake, despite the time.'

'Nothing wrong with that,' Sarah says. 'The cakes are over here, dear. Freshly baked this morning.'

She shows me to an area where the cakes are displayed in a plexiglass case and I have a hard time choosing, they all look so good. 'I think I'll try the lemon drizzle.'

'Good choice.' She cuts me a big slice and puts it on a tray along with our coffees.

We find a table next to the window overlooking the beach and sit opposite each other. While Stoker pours cream into his coffee and adds sugar, he says, 'Do you swim?'

That's a strange question to ask out of the blue. 'Yes, I do swim,' I reply. What I don't tell him is how I always wear a t-shirt over my swimsuit or bikini. And it's always a dark t-shirt so it won't get see-through when it's wet, revealing the ugly scars on my arms.

'Excellent.' He takes a sip of coffee.

'Are you going to tell me why?'

'Because that means I can show you something. Something really cool.'

'That's what all the boys say.'

He laughs and almost chokes on his coffee. 'No, that wasn't a line. There really is something I want to show you. I think you'll like it.'

'Sounds intriguing.'

'Tomorrow's Sunday so the bookshop is closed and the garage is closed and...the tide should be out at lunchtime...plus the weather forecast is good. How about tomorrow? You free?'

What would I be doing other than moping around the house eating junk food and watching TV?

'I'm sure I will be free around lunchtime.'

'Great. I'll come pick you up around eleven. You'll need a swimsuit and a towel. I'll bring everything else.'

'OK.' He seems really excited so I hope I'm going to like whatever it is he's going to show me.

I taste the lemon cake and it fills my mouth with tangy citrus flavors perfectly set off by the light sponge. 'Oh my God, this cake is amazing!'

He laughs. 'The perfect breakfast.'

'Don't knock it. You want to try some?'

'No thanks, I'll pass.'

'Well you're missing out.'

'No, I'm not. Sitting here with you is what I've been wanting since I first saw you.'

'Really? That time on the driveway? I have to apologize about that. I was tired and...'

'Don't apologize, you were really nice. That's why I tried to ask you out after we got back from Penzance.'

'What? Oh, you mean your 'show you around Promise

Cove' thing? Oh my God, I didn't realize, Stoker. I'm sorry.'

'Yes, that 'thing'. Anyway, here we are.'

I nod. 'Here we are.' And I can't think of any place I would rather be than here with him. He really does seem to be the perfect man. In a way that worries me because I feel like I should be pinching myself to make sure this isn't a dream. But all my dreams are nightmares so this can't be one of them.

'But there is a downside to us being here,' I say.

'What's that?'

'You didn't finish your painting.'

'Never mind that. I'm really not bothered about it.'

'But you came out there early to catch the dawn light and I took you away from it and now the dawn is over.'

'There's a dawn every day, you know.'

'Yes, I am aware of that fact.'

'Besides, I don't come out early to get the light necessarily. I told you, it's to avoid my dad.'

'You said he doesn't like you painting?'

'Yeah.'

'But you're old enough to decide what you want to do, so why go sneaking around behind his back? Why not just tell him?'

'It's more complicated than that. It hurts him when I do stuff like painting and drawing.'

'You're going to have to explain that a little more. It doesn't make sense.'

He takes a swallow of coffee and puts the cup down on

the table. 'I saw you at the cemetery the other morning. I couldn't speak to you because I was too upset. Do you know why I was there?'

'Your mother and brother are buried there. I saw their graves.'

'Yeah. James was my older brother and he was my hero. He wasn't just my hero, he was my dad's hero. James had a real talent for playing football...or soccer as you would call it...and he was probably going to go pro. He had a few interviews lined up with professional clubs. My dad is something of an old-fashioned man, or as I like to call it a neanderthal. So he loved that his son was a sports-man. James was everything Dad wanted in a son.'

I take a sip of coffee and prepare myself for what's coming next because I already know this story ends in tragedy. I've seen the graves.

'I was everything Dad didn't understand. I liked to read, to lose myself in fictional worlds and daydreams. My talents are artistic and creative, two things Dad thinks are worthless. So James didn't just become Dad's favorite son, he became the only son Dad understood. I know a lot of kids think they're misunderstood but I literally was. Paint-ing, drawing, reading...those things are alien to my dad. My mum tried to encourage me in the things I was inter-ested in but Dad told her she was turning me into a sissy. Real men like sports and cars and drinking as far as he's concerned.

'I learned enough about cars to be a mechanic in the garage and all three of us worked there for a while but even then Dad and James would spend all day talking about sports and basically ignore me.

'Then there was the car crash. Mum, James and I were in our Honda Civic on a clear spring evening coming home from a trip to the supermarket in Truro. As soon as we left Truro, my mum took the road that goes over the cliffs. There was a car broken down just around a bend. There was no way she could have seen it in time. The driver of that car was just getting out of his vehicle when we crashed into it. I was in the back seat and the impact threw me between the front seats and out through the windscreen. If we had been anywhere else, I would have landed on the ground at a high velocity and probably been killed, or at least broken a lot of bones. But because we were at a point where the road was close to the cliff edge, I was thrown over the cliff and into the sea.

'I remember landing in the water and being in incredible pain. The windscreen had cut my back and side to ribbons as I went through it and that made the salt water feel like acid in my wounds. I managed to swim to shore and drag myself up onto the beach but then I passed out. The paramedics found me there when they arrived at the scene.

'I found out later, when I was in the hospital, that Mum and James and the other driver had all been killed instantly.'

'That's terrible,' I say.

He nods. 'After the accident, Dad started drinking heavily every evening. He usually passes out but not before telling me how much of a disappointment I am to him. He wishes I had died in that crash and James had lived.'

'I'm sure that's not true.'

'Oh, it's true. He's told me as much.'

'He shouldn't say things like that.'

He shrugs. 'So that's why I keep my creative life hidden. It hurts him because it reminds him that I'm not James. It drives a wedge between us.'

'Stoker, you can't live your life pretending to be someone you're not.'

'I know that. It just makes things easier if I don't tell Dad when I'm painting. He's already lost James and when I'm doing something he doesn't understand, it makes him think he's losing me too. Maybe he is. We're such different people.'

'It sounds awful.'

'It is. My dad and I can't co-exist for much longer yet I feel so sorry for him. He lost his wife and son and now *he* feels lost.'

'You lost your mom and brother. He must see that it hurts you too.'

He shakes his head. 'No, not really.' He checks his watch. 'I need to get to the garage and open up. You want a ride home?'

'Yes, please.'

We say goodbye to Sarah as we leave and she tells us to come back soon. Stoker doesn't take my hand on the way back to the Land Rover and I'm surprised by how much I want him to.

When we're on the road climbing the cliffs toward Promise House, I look at him as he drives. Could this perfect but wounded boy really like me? Today feels so surreal and it's barely even begun.

He drops me at the house and reminds me that he'll be by tomorrow at eleven to pick me up. As he pulls out of the driveway, I wave to him and watch the Land Rover head back down the road.

I can hardly wait until tomorrow.

———

'You're kidding me!' Dell says. She's lying on her stomach in her bed in front of her webcam. I'm sitting in the living room at Promise House with my laptop on the coffee table in front of me. Dell's room with its familiar posters of rock bands and her collection of trolls on the dresser makes me wish I was there with my best friend.

There's a five hour time difference between here and there so for me it's ten o clock at night but or Dell it's only five in the evening. That makes me feel like we are living different lives and she is even further away from me than the thousands of miles. She's on a different time line, living her life out of synch with mine.

'It's all true,' I say.

'Oh my God, Amy, that is incredible! I knew the poor boy couldn't stay away for long but he's a faster mover than I thought. You have to admit, I called it.'

I let out a mock sigh. 'Yes, yes, you called it.' I pause.

'Did you really, though? You said he would call. He didn't. I just sort of bumped into him on the beach.'

'Don't you get it? That's even better. That means it's fate!'

'Oh boy.'

'And he's a painter. That means you have even more in common.'

'I don't paint, Dell.'

'No, but you write. Did you tell him you write poetry and stories? He'll love all that arty shit.'

'Shit?'

'You know what I mean. OK…arty stuff.'

'No, I didn't tell him. We really didn't talk all that long.'

'Because your body language said it all. Just take one of those journal notebooks you're always writing in. He'll totally love it. Two star-crossed artists fated to be together.'

'Dell!'

'Sorry. I'm just glad you're not hanging around in the house alone. It'll do you good to see new things and go places.'

'I don't have any of my journals here anyway, they're being shipped over on the boat with the rest of my stuff. It's going to be a couple of weeks before it gets here.' Apart from what I brought over on the plane in my luggage, my entire life has been packed in a single trunk which is being shipped over from Boston. There really isn't a lot in there except a lot of books and my writing journals. Stoker paints to escape the world for a little while and I write.

I started making stories up when I was ten years old and writing them down in handmade books that I glued together. I would draw covers for them and most of the stories involved knights and damsels in distress. The fact that my dad left us when I was ten years old probably has a lot to do with why I escaped into a fantasy world where the princess heroines had fathers who were noble kings. I was probably trying to make sense of things by creating these worlds where everything was orderly and right.

When I was twelve and we heard that my dad had died in a car crash in Michigan, hit by a drunk driver, my stories turned a lot darker. I'm sure that was when I first cut myself too. I was out in the street after hearing the news and I found a piece of shiny clear glass shining in the sunlight. I picked it up and without even thinking, I drew it across my arm.

I told my mom later that I had fallen over. I still don't know if she believed me or not.

'What do you mean you don't have a journal?' Dell asks, 'You own a store that friggin' *sells* them!'

'Do we sell them?'

'Yes, we sell them. You really have been daydreaming all this time. Go to the back on the right. There's a display there with journals, notebooks, pens and all kinds of stuff. Some fancy ones too.'

'OK, I'll take a look.'

Dell bursts into laughter and rolls around on her bed holding her stomach.

'What's so funny?'

'How can you own a store and not even know what it sells? Too funny.'

'Shut up.'

That makes her laugh even more.

She looks at her bedroom door then back at the camera. 'I have to go, Mom is calling me for dinner.'

'OK. I need to get some sleep anyway.'

'Yes, you do. Get plenty of beauty sleep for your big day tomorrow.'

I giggle. 'I will.'

'Love you.'

'Love you too.'

She signs out and I do the same, closing the lid of the laptop. I feel tired. The bookshop was quite busy today and getting up at six o clock this morning means the day was a long one.

And Dell is right, I do need my beauty sleep. I turn the lights out and head wearily upstairs. I don't know if tomorrow is going to be a big day as Dell says or not because I don't know what Stoker has planned. I didn't bring my swimsuit in my luggage so I went to the only women's clothing store in Promise Cove during my lunch break and bought a black bikini. And a black cotton shirt that is tight but has long sleeves. Perfect.

They're laid out on the top of my suitcase along with a beach towel and my blue jeans and a pair of sandals which I also got from the store today. They're wedges with blue canvas straps.

I also have bobby pins to put my hair up and a straw sun hat as well as sun cream and makeup in a little black nylon back that has a shoulder strap and is waterproof.

Whatever Stoker has planned involves water and since

he asked me if I could swim, I'm guessing I'm going to be getting wet tomorrow.

As I get into bed, I realize that if Dell could have heard my last thought, she would have added it to her list of double entendres. I laugh and lay my head on the pillow.

The moment I close my eyes, I drift into a dreamless sleep.

CHAPTER
NINE

AMY

Stoker arrives at exactly eleven, pulling onto the driveway in a black car and parking out front next to the Volvo. He gets out and I remind myself again that this handsome young man actually asked me out on a date today. A mysterious date for sure but still a date nonetheless. He's wearing a dark blue sleeveless t-shirt which displays tribal tattoos running down his muscular arms.

As I get closer, I can see that the intricate swirls and knots rendered in black ink are made up of celtic patterns and lines that loop eternally around each other. He also has on faded blue jeans with a black leather belt and the eagle buckle he was wearing when I first met him and a pair of black boots.

He looks really hot with his muscles and tattoos and intense gray eyes and I have to remind myself to act casual. I just want to grab him and pull him inside and taste those sensuous lips of his but we haven't even kissed yet and that might be too forward of me. I don't want to scare him off. I'm not sure what's come over me; I'm not used to having these thoughts. The last time I had these kinds of feelings about a guy was sometime never.

I have on my bikini beneath my jeans and the long-sleeved shirt. The wedges took some getting used to because I mainly wear pumps but a few circuits of Promise House helped me adjust to them. I'm wearing my sunglasses and sun hat, under which my hair is pinned up, as I go out to meet him. The little black bag is slung over my shoulder and all that's in it is the sun cream, a layer of which I've already applied, and a spare lipstick and my towel.

'Wow,' Stoker says when he see me, 'you look great!'

I smile and his compliment makes me feel taller than the wedges ever could. 'This your car?'

'Yeah, it's our Astra. My dad drives it mainly, which is probably why I there's a big scratch on the front passenger side panel. He sometimes drives it when he shouldn't.'

'You mean when he's been drinking?'

'Rarely, and not if I know about it. I probably need to hide the keys when he's drinking but I can't watch him all the time. Anyway, I had to leave the Land Rover at the garage in case he gets called out to an RTA.'

'RTA?'

'Road Traffic Accident. If there's a wreckage or a car

that can't be driven, we get called out by the police. It was Dad who got called out to the accident that killed Mum and James. The police didn't know who the victims were until he got there.'

'Oh my God, that's terrible!'

'Yeah. Anyway, shall we go? It's a lovely day.' He opens the passenger door and I get in, taking off my hat so I can fit inside. They really need to get larger cars in England. The Volvo is fine but this compact is way smaller than an American car.

Stoker slides into the driver's seat. He smells good, like he's wearing a cologne that's musky and spicy at the same time.

'So where are we going?' I ask.

'I can't tell you that until we get there. Where we are going is a secret place known only to a few.'

'Ooh, sounds very intriguing.'

He drives us along the cliff top road toward town and I think he's taking me to the main beach, which is really busy today with people on vacation. Kids run riot on the sand while their parents sit beneath big parasols and drink coffee from Thermos flasks. Stoker drives past.

'I thought we were going to the beach,' I say.

He shakes his head. 'Nope. Not that beach anyway. Today's adventure starts at another beach.' He drives through town, along Main Street, past Promise Books which now looks so familiar to me and is starting to feel like mine. The first few days, even though I love the place, I felt like I was trespassing on Aunt B's turf. Now I do feel as if it's my responsibility and my place.

Even if I didn't know we sell notebooks and pens.

Stoker takes us out of town and back up onto the cliff road then down a bumpy dirt track to a tiny cement parking area next to a little cove with its own sandy beach. There's no one here. The sun reflects off the calm sea and the air smells of salt and seaweed. Gulls cry in the distance. The rocks sweep up on either side, protecting the cove from the wind and from the sight of the thousands of tourists who come through Promise Cove every year.

'It's beautiful,' I say.

'It is,' he agrees, 'but this is only part of what I brought you here to see. Come on.' He grabs my hand and leads me down to the beach. We walk across the sand and this picture perfect place is made even more perfect because I'm here with Stoker and he's holding my hand. It just feels so right.

He leads me to the base of the cliff and behind a natural rock wall. 'We'll leave our shoes and clothes and stuff here.' He starts to unbuckle his belt and I want to just stand her and watch him but I have to get my own clothes off too so I pull at the buttons on my own jeans and slide them down my legs. I notice him glance over at me. I fold the jeans and put them on the sand next to my shoes and bag. I stow the sunglasses in the bag and use the weight of the bag to hold my hat on the sand so it won't blow away.

'What about your top?' Stoker asks.

'This stays on.'

He doesn't ask why. He puts his jeans with his boots and stands there in swimming shorts and the sleeveless t-shirt.

'What about the top?' I ask him.

'This stays on.'

Is he being weird with me because he thinks I'm being weird? I can't tell him why I'm not taking my top off an I can't let him see my scars. How to lose a guy in thirty seconds flat…make him think you're a psycho and show him how ugly your body is.

If he was being weird with me, it seems to have passed just as quickly. 'You ready?' he asks with a grin.

'Sure.'

He leads me back out from behind the rocks to the sandy beach and points at the side wall of the cove. 'See where the cliff goes out into the sea there?'

'Yeah.'

'We're going to swim around there…around that corner. Can you handle that?'

I nod. 'Yeah, no problem.'

'But first, you need to pick a pebble from the beach.'

'A pebble?'

'Yes. Just look around the water's edge and find one that speaks to you, one that draws you to it.'

'You're full of it. Is this a joke?'

He looks at me with those intense eyes and shakes his head. 'No, it's no joke. Just find a pebble.' He goes down to the water's edge himself and starts looking at the pebbles there, sifting through them with his fingers.

Alright, I'll play along.

I walk ankle-deep into the sea. The cool water feels good on my feet after the hot sand. Little pebbles of all different colors roll back and forth with the gentle waves. I see a blue one I like and grab it. Standing back up, I see Stoker approaching me. The sun hits his muscular arms, highlighting the curves of his broad shoulders and solid biceps. He holds out his hand to show me a little black shiny stone with flecks of dark green around its perimeter. 'Got mine,' he says.

I hold up my blue one between my thumb and forefinger. 'Is this OK?'

'Only you an answer that, Amy. It has to be the one you think is right. Did it stick out from all the others?'

'I guess so, yeah. It's pretty.'

'Then it's the right one.'

'When did you go all new age hippy?'

He grins and says, 'Ready for a swim? Don't drop your pebble in the sea.'

'I won't.'

'It's about half a mile to the end of those rocks. You sure you'll be OK?'

'I'm a strong swimmer.'

He nods and says, 'Follow me' and wades into the sea, taking his pebble with him. When he gets to thigh-depth, he launches himself forward and starts to swim in a breast stroke toward the far rocks.

I follow him and when I hit the water it takes my breath away because it's colder than I thought it would be. I swim out after Stoker, holding the little blue pebble trapped in the pad of my thumb. I have no idea what this is all about but I'm enjoying myself so far. The secret beach is gorgeous. Let's face it, just being with Stoker is exciting even if we were sitting at home. Being with him at a beautiful secret beach is all bonus extras.

The water gets deep really fast but it's crystal clear and as I swim I can see weeds and rocks on the bottom far below. Stoker is about ten feet ahead of me and he keeps looking over his shoulder to check I'm OK. This is the farthest I've swum in a long time but I feel fine and the pace he has set is a gentle one. I swim in his wake, my strokes falling into time with his, and the coldness of the water not bothering me at all now. I look back at the beach and it looks so far away. Stoker's black car looks tiny sitting in the parking area and I can't even see the rocks where we stowed our clothes.

I look ahead again and Stoker is rounding the edge of the rocks, swimming out of the cove and disappearing from my sight. A panic grips me. I'm so far from shore and he can't see me. What if I get cramp? My breathing increases not just because of the exertion of swimming but because I'm working myself up into a state of anxiety. 'Just breathe calmly,' I whisper to myself.

What sort of fish do they have in these waters? Are there sharks? No, there aren't any sharks in Cornwall except basking sharks and they're harmless to people. Just stay calm.

Stoker's voice call from beyond the rocks. 'You OK, Amy?'

I let out a big exhale. His voice is like an anchor. I feel calmer. Breathe. In. Out. Follow his voice. Steady strokes.

I swim around the rocks and he's there treading water, waiting for me. He looks so good.

'You alright?' he asks, looking concerned.

'I'm fine.'

'We're almost there.'

Almost where? There's nothing out here except deep water and rocks. I follow him a little farther along the cliff face then he heads for the rocks and climbs out onto them, smiling and waiting for me to join him.

A minute later, I'm standing on the rocks with him, the breeze cooling my skin. 'Nice view,' I say, shivering a little.

'I didn't bring you here to see the view. You still got your pebble?'

'Yeah.' I hold it up to show him.

'Follow me.' He walks a little way along the rocks then points to a cave above us. 'This is it.'

'A cave?'

'Not just any cave. This is the Cave of the Mermaid.'

'There's a mermaid in there? Now I *am* impressed.'

'I don't think anyone else knows about this cave. James and I found it a long time ago and we named it. You can't see it from land and you can't really see it from a boat either. We found it totally by accident when we were swimming out here and fooling around on the rocks.'

He clambers up and holds down his hand to help me. I take his hand and he pulls me up. He's strong. I climb the last few feet on my own and then I stand at the entrance of the Cave of the Mermaid.

Stoker is standing there grinning like a Cheshire cat. He points to the wall just inside the cave. In a natural alcove is a white stone statue of a mermaid. She's sitting on a rock combing her hair as mermaids do. The alcove goes back into the rock and there are pebbles of all shapes and sizes and colors scattered around the statue.

'You have to give your offering to the mermaid before you enter the cave,' Stoker says, placing his black pebble in the alcove. 'It's a rule that James made up and I always follow it.'

I put my blue pebble next to Stoker's. 'So all these were put here by you and James? You must have come here a lot.'

'Over the years, yes. We used a rubber dinghy to bring some stuff out here, including the mermaid which we got at a junk sale. The tide doesn't reach this high so it's all dry inside. Come on.' He picks up a flashlight from the ground and leads me back into the cave.

The ceiling is high enough that we can walk without stooping over. The flashlight picks out an alcove which Stoker reaches into and pulls out a lighter in a plastic zippy bag. He gets it out and uses the flashlight to find a candle sitting on a chrome candleholder. He lights it then finds more candles dotted around the cave and lights those too until the whole place is lit up.

The cave is maybe twenty feet wide by thirty feet long and at least ten feet high. In the far corner is a ring of stones set out to mark a fireplace. 'You have fires in here?'

'Yeah. There's a hole above there that takes the smoke out like a natural chimney. I burn duraflame logs that you get at the store instead of wood because they're easy enough to carry out here in watertight bags and they burn longer than wood.'

'What do you do out here?'

'Just sit and think mainly. Sometimes I draw. It's comfy, look.'

There are inflated air mattresses on the floor and fold-up chairs. There's even a small plastic collapsible table.

'It's amazing,' I say.

'I thought you'd like it.'

'Stoker.'

'Yes?'

'Could we have a fire? I'm kind of cold.'

'Of course!' He goes over to the fire circle and gets two fire logs from a stack by the wall. He places them inside the circle and uses the lighter on them. They start to burn slowly. I'm shivering. Swimming in the sea then standing in a cave is a good way to lose body heat.

'There are some blankets over there,' he says, pointing to a stack of blankets and pillows near the mattresses.

'Do you sleep here?'

'Sometimes. After I got out of hospital I used to come here at night and sleep here sometimes. I felt close to James here because we found this place together. This is probably the only thing we did together. He was into his sports and I was into painting but this place brought us together. He even named the mermaid. Her name's Mara.'

He looks around the cave. The flickering light from the fire dances over his arms, making the celtic bands seem to shift and writhe.

'I can't feel him here anymore. I know that he put some of those pebbles in the alcove and helped me build this ring of stones to make the fireplace but I can't feel his presence like I used to.'

I wrap a blanket around me and he says, 'Come over here by the fire. It's warmer.'

I sit next to him and he puts an arm around me. He makes me feel safe. I lean into him. 'Aren't you cold too?'

'A bit. The fire should catch in a minute.'

I look into his lovely gray eyes and for the first time in my life, I want to kiss someone. I'm not just going through the motions. I want it. I don't think I've ever wanted anything more.

Whether the thought causes a subtle shift in my body language or in my eyes, Stoker catches it and he leans forward slowly. I close my eyes and I feel his lips touch mine, softly at first then a little more firmly as our mouths meet and we taste each other for the first time.

He tastes like a mixture of clear sea and sharp mint. His lips work with mine perfectly and I feel his hand lift from my shoulder to the back of my head, his fingers in my pinned-up hair and tracing down the back of my neck, sending shivers down my spine that have absolutely nothing to do with being cold.

We break for a moment and he looks at me, his eyes roaming across every inch of my face as if he needs to remember every detail of me.

'Amy, I've wanted to do that since I met you.'

'Me too,' I admit, snuggling against his chest and looking into the fire.

'You warmer now?'

'A little.' I look back up to him and we kiss again, our mouths more familiar with each other now and moving together in unison. This time when we break, I put a hand on his shoulder and trace the strong curve of the muscle down over his bicep and forearm until I reach his hand. He intertwines his fingers with mine and we sit in front of the fire in the cave holding hands, each lost in our own thoughts.

I feel much warmer now.

———

Stoker

She's amazing. I had to think long and hard before bringing her out her because I'm the only living person who knows about the Cave of the Mermaid. Now I'm sharing that secret with Amy and I'm so glad I did. I know I can trust her. I don't know what it is about her but I just feel so comfortable with her and I feel as if I've known her forever.

It isn't just physical attraction, it goes beyond that. But when she came out of Promise House in those high shoes with that sunhat and shades on, her tight black top and jeans revealing her figure, I was blown away. The bikini bottoms were almost too much for me to handle. Great legs. Great ass.

It's probably a good thing she didn't take her top off because I don't think I could stay sane if she was walking around in just her bikini. Also it makes me less conspicuous for keeping my t-shirt on. Amy thought I was being arsey when I said it stays on but I wasn't saying that because she'd said the same thing; my top was never coming off. I never take it off. Not after the accident and the scars it left on my back and left side. Nobody wants to see that.

I can still taste her on my lips. She tastes sweet like cherry. And she feels so good leaning against me like this. I know she's been through a lot in her life and I just want to hold her and say it's all going to be OK because I'll protect her.

And maybe she's the one who's going to save me without even knowing it. Three times now I've left the house when Dad went on a bad drinking session and three times I've done things I'm not proud of. I can't help myself. I have to release the pent up anger somehow.

It's a good thing Dad doesn't know about the arrests because he'd fly off the handle. Or maybe if he did know about them he'd think I was more of a 'man'. They don't make me feel like a man, they make me feel ashamed. I've hurt people and it isn't right.

When I'm around Amy, I don't feel that anger. Even just thinking about her makes me feel calm. I want to feel calm. I want to feel like I do right now, with her in my arms and the taste of her on my lips.

Perfection.

I bend my head to hers and she comes up to meet me, our lips locking. I don't think a kiss has ever tasted this good. I place my fingers on the back of her neck and she shivers. Her skin is so soft and smooth and warm beneath my touch despite her saying she's cold. I venture into her mouth with my tongue and she reciprocates. She tastes so fucking good.

All of the girls in my life up until now have been tourists. It's easy and it's simple and it has a built-in time limit. They come for a couple of weeks on holiday then they're gone. No one expects anything more and everyone knows what they're signing up to. No ties. Definite end time. Fun and romantic while it lasts and maybe a few interesting stories to tell your friends when you get back from your holiday.

That was my life.

Every summer.

Not any more. For the first time, I want something else. I want it to last. I don't want fun and frolics on the beach while checking the date behind a girl's back and thinking, 'she'll be gone soon. Then I'll move on to the next one.' No more of that.

I don't know how Amy has affected me like this but it's just the way it is. I knew it from the moment I saw her on the porch of her house. Destiny. Maybe. I don't know but it feels like destiny.

I close my eyes and feel the warm glow of the fire on me.

Amy is quiet in my arms and I wonder if she's asleep. If not, she's very content and just enjoying this closeness.

Perfection.

———

Amy

. . .

I think I drifted off to sleep. I open my eyes and the fire is burning low. Stoker is leaning back against the cave wall with his eyes closed.

'Stoker, are you awake?'

He opens one eyes and peers at me. 'Of course.'

'Liar.' I punch him on the chest playfully.

He grins. 'I'm awake now.'

'What time is it?'

He picks up the flashlight and shines it at a spot on the wall where an old pocket watch dangles from an outcropping of rock. The watch says it's almost two o clock.

'Almost three.'

'The watch says almost two.'

'The clocks went forward one hour in spring. I didn't adjust it.'

'Maybe we should be getting back.'

'Yeah, we should. It's a rough swim out of here at high tide.'

'What?'

'Don't worry, that isn't yet. I timed our visit for minimum hassle from the sea.'

'Did you count on falling asleep?'

'No. I didn't count on kissing either.' He grins.

'Want another one?'

'Yes, it'll give me strength for the swim back to the beach.'

I lean forward and kiss him. He kisses me back and the contact sends tingles through my body. We break and I'm almost panting. That was passionate one. They're increasing in passion every time. I'm not sure how long it's going to be before things get hotter and I'm not sure how long I can wait.

In an effort to keep some decorum, I stand up and say, 'Come on, we need to get back.' I need a hot shower or a soak in the tub. Falling asleep wearing wet clothes was not a good idea, fire or not.

Stoker gets up and kicks sand over the fire. He starts extinguishing the candles one by one until we're in blackness illuminated only by the flashlight. We walk out into the sunshine. It warms me a little but the thought of getting back into the cold water chills me inside.

Clambering down the rocks is easier than getting up them. We reach the water's edge and the cold sea washes over my feet. The thought of immersing my body in the deep water frightens me.

Stoker senses something is wrong and takes me hand. 'It's just a short swim back to the beach and we have towels and I'll put the heater on full blast in the car and take you home. How does that sound?'

I nod.

'OK. On three we'll jump in. Keep holding my hand. 1…'

I prepare myself for the shock of all that cold water washing over me.

'2…'

He tightens his grip on my hand.

'3…'

We jump and suddenly I'm under the water, hearing it

rushing around my ears and pulling me down. I kick out with my legs and feel my face break the surface. I take a breath and tread water, my body almost numb from the chill.

Stoker is beside me. 'The sooner we get moving the warmer we'll be.' I can tell he's cold too but he's trying not to show it. He waits for me to start off then he swims along next to me. We round the rocks and swim into the cove and I can see the beach but it looks too far away. I'll never make it will I? If only I wasn't so cold.

I try to think of something warm. A hot bowl of chicken soup. No I need something warmer. A bathtub full of hot water and strawberry-scented bubbles. I imagine sinking down into it and feeling the hot water on my skin. I could put my face under and let the warm water bring feeling back to my lips and cheeks. I imagine sliding beneath the strawberry bubbles.

Somewhere in the distance I hear Stoker shout my name. He sounds panicked. I don't know why. It's calm in the bathtub. Peaceful.

Then suddenly I'm coughing and there's cold water in my mouth and throat and I'm being dragged out of the bathtub. No, not out of the bathtub...over the sand. The sand of the beach. Stoker has me by the arm and he's pulling me out of the sea. I feel so cold. He sets me down on the sand and I balance precariously on my hands and knees while I cough and splutter and spit the salty water from my mouth.

Stoker is standing above me, hands on his hips while he tries to catch his breath.

'I'm sorry,' I manage to say.

'Nearly lost you there. I'm sorry Amy. I should never have taken you out so far.'

'I can handle it. It was just so cold.'

He disappears for a moment then comes back with our stuff from the rocks. He drapes my towel over me.

'When you're ready, we can get in the car and I'll put the heater on.'

I get up shakily. 'I'm ready.'

He takes my hand and we head for the car.

'I feel like such an idiot,' he says.

'You feel like an idiot? I'm the one who almost drowned. You saved my life. Thank you.'

'You wouldn't have been out there in the first place if it wasn't for me.'

'I enjoyed it. Really. It's just the last part that could have been better.'

He laughs but I can see he's shaken by what happened. He helps me into the car, putting my towel around me before closing the door and getting in himself. He twists the air temperature dial to its maximum heat setting and puts the fan on full blast.

He starts the engine but before he drives away from the secret cove, he says, 'Promise me something, Amy.'

'What?'

'That you'll choose where we go on our next date.'

I smile. 'I'm sure I can handle that. I promise.'

He gives me a little kiss then puts the car into gear and heads back to the main road.

RESERVED

AMY

I open the front door and say, 'Wow! Don't you look amazing?'

Stoker stands there in a dark blue suit with a crisp white shirt underneath and a powder blue tie. He's arranged his hair into a sort of side-parting and he's even wearing black shoes instead of his usual boots. In his hands is a bouquet of flowers. He hands them to me and shuffles his feet like he's embarrassed.

'Thank you! Lilies, my favorite. Well come in, don't stand out there on the porch. I'm almost ready.'

'You look amazing, Amy.'

I'm wearing a brand new black dress along with a thin black cardigan that covers my upper arms nicely that I got from a store in Penzance. I took a drive out there to see something more than Promise Cove for a change. I smile and say, 'Thanks. I just need to get my earrings.' I go up to my room and hunt through my jewellery box for my best pair of gold earrings.

After our adventure at the Cave of the Mermaid, I was going to suggest going to Pierre Moir's, a fancy restaurant just outside of Promise Cove, for our second date. But because Promise Cove is so small, our second date turned out to be lunch in one of the Italian places on Main Street after I bumped into Stoker just as I was closing the shop for a break.

Then our third date was coffee and cake in Sarah's after we crossed paths there one morning.

Our fourth date happened when I saw Stoker on the beach one morning painting the cliffs and rocks he had wanted to paint when I ran into him before. This time I let him paint and I sat on the sand and watched him. When he was done, he handed me the painting and told me it was a gift from him to me. I hung it up in the kitchen where I would see it every morning as I ate breakfast.

Our fifth date was a burger at a fast food chain after Stoker called me just as I was about to close for the evening, saying he was hungry.

And our sixth date consisted of Chinese takeaway which we ate on the floor of Promise Books after closing time.

So four weeks later we finally get to go to Pierre Moir's for our seventh date. I got Stoker to make a reservation and when he told me the place had a reputation for being expensive, I assured him I was worth it. He told me he was going to come suitably attired but I didn't know he'd look this great in a suit. I can't wait to go to the swankiest restaurant around with the hunkiest guy I've ever met.

I put the earrings in and go back downstairs. Stoker is waiting in the hallway looking uncomfortable in his smart clothes but deliciously adorable nonetheless.

'You could have had a seat in the living room,' I say.

'No, it's OK. I don't mind waiting here.'

'Silly boy.'

We get in the Astra and he turns right into the cliff road. 'Where are we going again?'

'You know where. And don't worry about the cost, we'll go dutch.'

'OK, that sounds fair. I did buy you that pasta in Luigi's that lunchtime after all.'

'Oh, really? And I bought you coffee and a big slice of walnut cake in Sarah's.'

'I'm sure this place is very nice. I'm just not sure I'll fit in there.'

'Don't worry about it. You look hot. Every waitress will be swooning.'

'I don't want every waitress to be swooning, I just want you to be swooning.'

'I'm swooning, believe me.'

———

Pierre Moir's restaurant is attached to a five star hotel called Le Chambre and it's visited by the top business men and women and their associates. I feel a little hesitant myself as we pull into the parking lot and see the opulent chrome and glass building which seems out of place in this area but has been built away from the towns for just that reason. It's like a country club and has its own golf course and horse riding facilities. When I chatted with customers in the bookshop and told them I was going to eat at Pierre Moir's, none of the had ever been here but they had all heard how wonderful the place was.

Stoker finds a spot to park the car. His little Astra seems out of place among the Jaguars and high-spec sports cars. We link arms and head for the restaurant entrance. 'I hope they don't discover we're just country bumpkins,' Stoker says through the side of his mouth as we approach the door.

I giggle and he holds the door open for me. Inside there's soft jazz piano playing, not from speakers but from an actual pianist sitting at a grand piano on the far side of the room. There's a low hum of chatter and the place is very busy. Everyone is dressed up.

The smell of food makes my stomach rumble with anticipation. I didn't eat lunch today because I knew we were coming here. It's eight thirty now and I am hungry enough to eat one of the tables.

The maitre d comes over smiles at us. 'Good evening. What name is it, please?'

'Stoker.'

'Merci.' He consults a list and says, 'Right this way, please.'

He shows us to a table at the edge of the room, and

holds out my chair for me. I sit and he unfolds our napkins, placing them on our laps. 'May I get you the wine list?'

'Yes, please,' I say.

Stoker is about to object but I throw him a glance. The Maitre d says, 'A waiter will be with you shortly,' and leaves.

'I can't have wine, I'm driving.'

'True. I agree. No drinking and driving.'

'So you're going to have a glass of wine while I'm on soft drinks all night? Great.' He sticks out his tongue at me.

'No, we're going to have a bottle between us.'

'But I just said I won't drink and drive.'

'Very commendable. I agree.'

'What's going on, Amy?'

I laugh, unable to keep my secret in any longer. 'Well you made us reservations for the restaurant, right?'

'Yes.'

'And I made us reservations for the hotel.'

'What? Really?'

I nod. 'We aren't in any hurry to get back. And tomorrow is Sunday so we aren't even in a hurry to get back in the morning.'

'You are sneaky with your little secrets. How much is the room?'

'Let's just say you'd better be worth it.'

He grins and takes my hand over the table. 'I really… I've really loved being with you, Amy.'

'You make it sound like it's all over. Is there something I should know?'

He laughs. 'No, I'm just having a great time.'

'Me too, Stoker.'

The waiter appears with the wine list. Stoker looks down it and says, 'How about an Asti Spumante?'

'Err…OK?'

'It's a sparkling white Italian wine. You'll like it. It's fizzy and sweet like you.'

I laugh. 'Fizzy and sweet, huh? Sure, let's try it.'

———

The meal was delicious. I had sea bass with potatoes and vegetables and Stoker had steak with fries. The Asti Spumante was lovely. Stoker had been right, I did like it. We skipped dessert, both if us saying we were full but really I think we were both ready to go to our room.

Stoker slides the keycard into the slot and pushes open the door. The lights come on automatically and we step inside.

'Oh my God.'

The room is huge, more like a suite. There's a lounge area with a plush sofa and easy chair and a flatscreen TV on the wall. There's a fireplace with little fake logs behind a glass screen and a computer on a desk.

The bedroom has a four poster bed which is probably the largest bed I have ever seen in my life. It's not only large, it's high and I think I'm going to have to climb up into it.

The mini bar is in the bedroom, as well as a small glass-fronted refrigerator that has soft drinks and a drink-making station with a kettle and tea and coffee.

A door off the lounge leads to the bathroom, which has a jacuzzi, a bathtub and a separate shower. The toilet is in its own separate room.

'This place is amazing,' Stoker says. 'Let's live here.' He takes off his jacket and drapes it over the back of a chair. He looks so good in the white shirt and blue tie and dark trousers.

'As tempting as that sounds, I don't think we can afford it. You should see what it costs for just one night.'

'Like I said, if you want me to pay…'

'No, I don't. And like I said, you'd better be worth it.'

He smiles and goes to the mini bar. 'Drink?'

'No, I'm good.' And I am good. Considering what we're about to do I feel amazingly relaxed. We both know our relationship has come to this point. It just feels so natural.

But there is still one small hurdle to get over. One last thing that could make or break tonight. I do feel nervous about that. Maybe I should get it over with otherwise it's going to be hanging over me.

I turnout the main lights and turn on the lamp on the nightstand. It makes the room gloomy but that's how I need it to be if I'm going to do this.

Stoker looks at me as if he's about to say something then sees my face and thinks better of it. 'What's up, Amy?'

'I need to talk to you. I need to show you…I…I need to

tell you something. Before any of…this.' I gesture to the bed.

'OK. You can tell me anything, you know that.'

I kick of my shoes and climb up onto the bed, kneeling there hugging myself. This is so going to turn him off me but I can't sleep with him and then have him find out later. Sure we could turn the lights out but what about when morning comes? I could wear something to cover my arms but isn't that a lie? I have to tell him before we sleep together. It's only fair.

He climbs onto the facing me. 'What is it, Amy. Is it that you're a…virgin?'

'No, I'm not a virgin.' One time. With Martin Classman. I thought that if I slept with him I would finally feel some-thing like lust or love. Wrong.

'What is it then?' He reaches out and his hand cups my cheek. I feel like crying. If he can't handle this, it will be too big a thing for us to get over. He's the best thing that ever happened to me and I don't want to lose him. I can't handle losing him.

He notices my hesitation and says, 'Hey, Amy, what-ever it is it can't be that bad.'

A tear falls unbidden from my left eye and rolls down my cheek and over his hand. 'It is,' I say.

'Take your time,' he says, 'we have all the time in the world.'

But all the time in the world wouldn't heal the scars on my arms. I'm permanently damaged. Ugly forever.

I take a deep breath and begin. 'When I was born, my

mom and dad and Aunt B all lived together in Promise House. It was plenty big enough for all of us and although my mom and dad weren't married, we all lived as one big family. Mom and Aunt B ran the bookshop and Dad worked selling computer systems to big companies and managing the projects to install the systems and train the staff.

'When I was five, he got a really great job offer from Boston to go work in America. He took it. There were a lot of arguments in the house at that time, some of them I can remember, because Mom didn't want to live abroad and leave her sister. Eventually she relented and we emigrated to America. She loved my dad and she couldn't stand the thought of them being apart and me being without a father.

'Things were good for five years...or at least they seemed to be good. Dad's job was great and I did well at school, even though I was always a misfit. Mom made a lot of friends and she even taught an English Lit class at a night school.

'When I was ten, my dad left us. He just went and left us. My mom didn't know what to do. She couldn't come back here because she didn't want to disrupt my schooling so she got a job at the power company in the offices. After he left, my emotions became suppressed to such a degree that I found it hard to feel anything. It was probably some safety mechanism inside me...don't have any emotions and you can't get hurt. But I started to live my life with a numbness inside.

'Two years later, we heard that my dad had been hit by a drunk driver and killed instantly. On that day, I went out into our street and I knew I should feel something. My father had just been killed and I was standing outside feeling nothing. No sadness, no pain. That safety mechanism inside me wouldn't let me experience anything.

'I saw a piece of glass on the sidewalk and I picked it up and looked at the sharp edge. I remember sitting there looking at it for a long time and thinking one thought: this can make me feel. Using this piece of glass, I could feel pain but I would be in control of it. I wasn't in any danger of being hurt emotionally because I would be in control.

'So I cut myself.

'I dragged the glass across my upper right arm and then I felt the pain that I knew I should be feeling. My daddy had just died. I wept.'

Stoker strokes my cheek with his thumb and I realize more tears are streaming down my face. 'I'm sorry,' I say, grabbing a tissue from the nightstand and wiping my eyes.

'There's no need to be. It sounds like you had a terrible time. It isn't your fault for finding a way to cope that involved hurting yourself like that.'

'It didn't end there, Stoker. That was just the beginning. Even though cutting myself with that piece of glass let me release my emotions about my dad, the emotional numbness returned afterward.

'So every time something happened that I thought required an emotional response from me, I cut myself. It was the only way I could release the emotional response I thought was required. If a boy at school was nasty to me, I came home and cut myself so I could cry. If I got a bad grade on my homework, I cut myself. It was the only way I could feel like a normal human being.

'My mom met Frank and we moved in with him and his daughter Julie. My life got a lot worse. Julie hated me. She was older than me and she spent the whole time bullying me. Frank was distant from me. He had no interest in me, any more than I had in him. All the time I was having such a hard time, I didn't realize that Mom was spiralling into depression. I think Frank ignored it, hoping it would just go away.

'A year ago, it did go away. Mom cut herself too. But just twice. Once down each wrist.'

'Amy, I'm so sorry.'

I wipe tears from my eyes. 'We all have our share of tragedy. You've had yours. But the way I handled it all through my life has left scars, Stoker. Physical scars. By the time Mom died, I was an expert at cutting myself. I wasn't using glass anymore, I had razor blades and iodine and bandages. I never showed my arms to anyone, not even Dell.

'But if you and I are going to be intimate, I can't let you sleep with me not knowing what I really look like.'

'Amy, it doesn't…'

'No, don't say it doesn't matter because it does matter. I want to be yours completely and that means I can't hide myself from you.'

He looks at my arms, still covered with the sleeves of the cardigan. 'Amy, if you think this is going to change anything, you're wrong.'

'You can't say that until you've seen them.'

He raises himself up a little on his knees and he places his hands on the edges of the cardigan. He gently pushes the fabric down my arms. As the first white line is revealed, I close my eyes, knowing that there are many more ugly lines crisscrossing below that one. Stoker pushes the sleeves all the way to my elbows. I'm totally exposed to him now. All of the ugliness bared before his eyes.

He leans forward and kisses the scar on my right shoulder. Then he moves down to the next ugly line and kisses that too. 'I want to kiss away all your pain,' he whispers, pressing his lips against every scar I have ever inflicted upon myself since I was twelve years old.

By the time he moves to my other arm, I am sobbing with relief and joy.

He finishes kissing my arms and looks into my eyes. How have I found him? How have I found the most caring, adorable man in the world?

'There's no need to hide yourself, Amy. Never hide yourself from me.' He loosens his tie and pulls the knot until it falls open. He begins to unbutton his shirt and says, 'Now it's my turn. I told you when I was thrown from the car, the glass cut me along my back and side. I have scars too.'

He opens the shirt and all I can see is his flawlessly muscled chest and the tight abs I saw the first time we met. Then he pulls the shirt off and throws it to the floor and I can see the healed scars running down his side. He turns slightly to reveal the lines down his back. They aren't hideous and I don't find them ugly at all. They are a part of Stoker and I can't find any part of him ugly.

He cups my face with his hands again, his thumbs stroking my tear-stained cheeks gently. 'We both have reminders of our pasts that we've kept hidden. But there's no need for that anymore.'

He leans forward and his lips meet mine. We kiss with an urgency that comes from having shared our secrets and now needing to share a physical need for each other. My hands go to his strong shoulder and his muscles feel hard and solid beneath his taut skin. He strokes my arms as our lips move together and his fingers trace carelessly over the scars, the light contact rendering every tragic memory associated with each scar harmless. All the tragedies written on my skin are part of the road that has led me to this moment on the bed with Stoker. I wouldn't change any of it. The road has been difficult but this destination feels perfect.

Stoker's lips move to my neck, sending shivers through my whole body as he places little ghost kisses over the sensitive flesh and moves down to my shoulder. His hands are on the sides of my dress, sliding around to the back in search of the zipper. I feel like all of my nerves have come alive and the signals they are sending to my brain are like delicious bright sparks of pleasure.

He finds the zipper and pulls it down slowly, his fingers stroking down my bare back. I press my body against him, my breasts touching the hard muscles of his chest. He pulls gently on my dress and it slips from my shoulders. I take my hands off his shoulders for a moment to allow the straps to pass over my arms. 'Let me get this off properly,' I whisper.

I slide off the bed and stand up, wriggling my hips to allow the dress to fall to the floor. My black panties and strapless bra barely cover my body but I want to show Stoker all of me because there are no secrets between us now.

His hands go to my sides as I climb back onto the bed and we kiss again, hard and deep with our tongues playing together. My whole body feels ultra-sensitive to every touch of Stoker's fingers as they stroke down over my hips and thighs. I gasp at the sensations building up inside my body and I feel like I'm losing control but I love it. It's a new experience for me because I spend all my time unable to feel emotions unless I cut myself but now it's like a floodgate has opened and I'm drowning in feelings.

My hands go to his trousers, fumbling at the button and catch that keep them closed. He helps me and with a simple one-handed manoeuvre he has unfastened the pants. My hand delves inside and I feel his hardness against my fingers. He groans and I stroke him slowly, trying to enflame the same feelings in him as he has sparked in me.

He unhooks my bra and removes it slowly, as if savoring the anticipation of seeing what lies beneath. As he uncovers my breasts, his mouth goes to the engorged nipples and suck them gently, making me arch my back and whimper. My hands work on him more firmly, squeezing and teasing and making him breathe harder, his breath arousing the hard tips of my breasts.

His kisses lay a warm trail of sensation down my stomach to the hem of my panties. He takes them between his thumb and forefinger and slides them down my thighs. I'm totally revealed to his gaze, a gift to him waiting to be claimed.

'Please, Stoker,' I whisper, 'I can't wait any longer.'

He slides off the end of the bed and removes his trousers and stands there naked for a moment. The fact that he is excited by me, scars and all, makes me feel a liberating sense of relief. Stoker reaches inside his jacket on the chair and brings out a foil packet. As he opens it he says, 'I've been carrying this around since last week.'

He comes back onto the bed his warm body pressing against mine from thigh to chest. I've never felt so close to anyone. I never want to feel this close to anyone but him.

His lips come down to mine and I am lost in his kiss as he enters me. We groan together and experience the most intimate coupling two souls can share.

I hold him to me, my hands stroking down his back, along the scars.

He kisses my neck and my shoulders and arms and he drives himself deep inside me.

I'm drowning in a sea of pleasure.

And when he cries out and explodes within me, I explode with him, my inner muscles locking him inside my center.

And I realize I am sobbing with the glorious exultation of release.

———

Stoker

She lies sleeping next to me, her breathing calm and deep. We lay together for hours after we had sex and Amy fell asleep on my chest. I stroked her hair and enjoyed the feel of her body pressed against me, feeling her chest rise and fall with her breathing as we cuddled. When my arm went dead, I moved her slightly to her side of the bed and lay here watching her.

The blanket has fallen from her shoulder slightly, revealing some of the scars she was so afraid of me seeing. They are part of her; they tell her story. Just as mine tell of my own personal tragedy.

I feel a bond with Amy that surprises me in its intensity. This is no summer fling. I've never felt this way for any girl. Ever.

I settle down in the bed and place an arm around Amy's waist.

She's very different from the frightened girl who stood on the porch of Promise House over a month ago. She's come out of her shell, developed an attractive confidence.

I liked her then when I first saw her but now I am falling for her hard. It's a new feeling for me and I'm not sure how I'm supposed to handle it. One day at a time seems like the best idea.

Settling against her naked body, I kiss her shoulder lightly so as not to wake her and I join her in the land of dreams.

SUSPICION

AMY

On Monday afternoon, I sit in the swivel chair behind the counter replaying my encounters with Stoker over and over in my head. The climb up the cliff trail where he first took my hand get a lot of repay value, and so does standing at the top of the trail feeling the sea breeze cool on my face while Stoker continued to hold my hand. Our first kiss in the cave was amazing and I feel touched that he would let me into his secret life so soon after we met. And the night in the hotel room was amazing.

The bell over the door rings and I look up to see Peter Macbeth coming into the store. He nods as he comes through the door and comes over to the counter. 'Good afternoon, Miss Anderson. Looks like we might get a storm tonight.'

'Good afternoon, Detective. Yes, I think you're right.' Dark storm clouds lay across the sky like an ominous warning of something to come.

'I have some news for you. We're abandoning our investigation. There isn't enough evidence to suggest anything other than you aunt somehow fell from that path. I thought you'd want to know.'

'Thank you.'

'I also thought you'd be happy with that news, I know how shocked you were the other day when I said we were investigating her accident.'

'Aunt Beth is still dead. Knowing it was an accident doesn't change that.'

'I'm sorry for your loss. Truly. I know the police force might seem faceless and uncaring to some but we see victims of tragedy every day and the hardest part of our job is getting used to it.'

'I'm not sure I could do a job that made me desensitized to people's suffering, Detective.'

He nods slowly in agreement. 'You're probably right. Do you mind if I buy some more books while I'm here?'

'No, of course not. That's what the shop is for.'

He smiles and walks to the stack of detective novels.

I watch him as he picks through the old paperbacks and I wonder if I should tell him my own theory on Aunt B's death. Is it better that everyone thinks she had an accident when I think the committed suicide? Does it even make a difference? As I said to Macbeth, she's still dead either way. Nothing is going to bring her back now. All of this later investigation isn't to help the dead any, it's so we the living can make sense of what happened and continue our lives with some sort of closure.

But if I know the truth, isn't telling the police the right thing to do? Do I know the truth? My theory is based on circumstantial evidence just as much as theirs is based on a lack of it.

Macbeth chooses two novels and brings them to the counter. 'Is your assistant not working today?'

'You mean Dell? She's gone back to America.'

'Oh, I see. She seemed like a nice girl.'

'Yeah, she's my best friend.'

'It must be hard having a friend so far away.'

'It is. Definitely.'

I ring up his purchase and he hands me a five pound note. 'Keep the change.' He turns for the door.

He opens it and the bell rings and he's about to step out onto the street.

'Detective Macbeth.'

He stops and faces me. 'Yes?'

'Have you considered that Aunt Beth might have… committed suicide?'

He comes back inside and closes the door. 'Does something in particular make you say that?'

'It's probably nothing.' It isn't nothing; it's something that doesn't fit, doesn't make sense. It means something.

'You can tell me whatever you like, Amy. What might seem trivial to you could fit with other evidence and break the case.'

'It's just that. The day before she…died…Aunt B put her cat into a cattery. It's as if she knew she no one would be able to look after him until I got here a week later.'

'You mean like making sure her affairs were in order?'

'Yes. If she was…killed…then that part doesn't make sense. If she was in danger, she wouldn't just put her cat somewhere out of the way, she'd call the police. I know Aunt Beth. She wouldn't hesitate to call you. And there's no reason for anyone to hurt her. But there *is* reason to suspect that she might have ended her own life.'

'Really? Go on.'

'My mother…Aunt Beth's sister…did the same thing a year ago. Took her own life, I mean.'

'I'm sorry. I didn't know that.'

'It happened in America. The point is, I've read a lot of information about depression and anxiety and it is possible for it to be a genetic trait, a misbalance of chemicals in the brain. With my mom taking her own life just a year ago, it makes it statistically more likely that my aunt could have done the same thing. She could have the same condition.'

He raises an eyebrow. 'So if this is true, you could have that same condition yourself.'

'I've battled with depression for most of my life, Detective.'

He thinks for a moment then says, 'The cat angle interests me. We knew your aunt had a cat because one of her friends told us so when we interviewed her. When we couldn't find Mr…Tibbles?'

I nod. 'Mr Tibbles.'

'We assumed he was just outdoors. But if he was put into a cattery the day before the accident, we need to know why and who put him in there.'

'It was Aunt Beth who put him in the cattery.'

'Are you sure?' He pulls a little black notebook and a pencil from the inside of his coat and scribbles a few notes.

'Yes, she signed the form. I saw her signature myself.'

'OK, and what is the name of he cattery?'

'Meow Meow.'

'That's in Penzance.'

'You know it?'

'With a name like Meow Meow, I'm not likely to forget it. I've walked past it many times. Is there a branch near to Promise Cove?'

'No, Mr Tibbles was at Penzance.'

'There are places much closer where she could have put the cat. Very strange.'

'That's what I told Stoker. It doesn't fit.'

'Stoker? Dean Stoker?'

'Yes,' I say, surprised that he knows Stoker's name.

He poises the pencil over the notebook. 'Tell me more about your relationship with Dean Stoker.'

His sudden change in demeanor makes me wary. 'Do you know Stoker?'

'Yes, Dean Stoker is known to us.'

'Why? I don't understand.'

'Dean Stoker has been arrested a couple of time for public disturbance. Fighting.'

I remember the cuts on his knuckles. I had tried to tell myself that he could have got them working on engines.

'But what interests me more,' Detective Macbeth continues, 'is that we interviewed Mr Stoker just after your aunt's death.'

'What? Why?'

'Our lab technicians found traces of engine oil on your aunt's clothing. At the same time, our officers discovered links between Dean Stoker and your aunt.'

'Links? What kind of links?' I can't believe I'm hearing this and my heart is beating like a hammer in my chest.

'They had contact on a few occasions.'

'What do you mean by contact?'

'We aren't sure exactly but they knew each other and the oil was enough circumstantial evidence for us to visit Dean. At the time, he had a satisfactory explanation for the oil on your aunt's clothing. Her car had broken down that day. The exhaust fell off while she was driving along the Sea Road. We have witnesses to that fact. It could explain the oil if she picked up the broken piece of pipe or went to look under her car.'

'That doesn't sound like Aunt Beth. She'd call a tow truck.'

'She did. She called Dean Stoker. He went out there in his Land Rover and towed the car to his garage. He showed it to us. It was parked behind the garage. The silver Volvo you've been driving. He'd fixed it and was going to return it early the next morning to your aunt but by then she…had her accident.'

He shakes his head. 'So the oil stain could have been picked up from her own car or while she was in Stoker's

Land Rover. He might even have touched her to help her climb into the vehicle. It led us nowhere.'

I'm stunned into silence. Stoker said nothing about this at all.

'So what is your relationship with Dean Stoker, Amy? It's interesting that he's made contact with you.'

Made contact? What is Macbeth suggesting…that Stoker might have murdered Aunt Beth and is returning to the scene of the crime to see how much I know? I don't believe it. I won't believe it. I refuse to believe it.

'He brought the car back to the house. That's all. And we had coffee.' I don't tell him any more than that.

He writes in the notebook. 'You say you had coffee. Did he initiate that contact?'

'No, I just ran into him one morning totally by chance.'

'Where was this?'

'On a beach. I was on the cliffs. I just saw him there.'

'What beach was this?'

The beach where Aunt Beth was found.

I don't know. I was just out walking.

And Stoker was painting on the beach where they found her body. *Returning to the scene of the crime?*

And who suggested coffee?

'He did. We went to a beachside coffee shop in town.'

'Sarah's?'

'Yes.'

'What did you talk about?'

'Nothing really, just passed the time of day. Small talk.'

I don't mention anything else. I feel like I'm betraying Stoker just telling Macbeth this much.

He makes a note then says, 'Did he mention your aunt in any way while you were there? Did he bring up her accident?'

'No.'

'Amy, I'm going to re-open the investigation.'

I sigh. 'Fine. But I really don't think Stoker could have anything to do with this.'

'I'll let you know the moment we find out anything.'

'But I wasn't telling you this because I think Aunt Beth was murdered, I was telling you because I think she committed suicide. The fact that she made arrangements for her cat only fits the suicide theory.'

'We'll investigate both avenues. Thank you for the information.'

He leaves the shop and I sit there wishing I had never opened my mouth at all. The police interviewed Stoker over Aunt B's accident and he never told me, never even mentioned it in passing. I don't understand what's going on. Why is Stoker being secretive and what is this 'contact' he had with my aunt? I knew there was a connection there when I first met him and he said he had fixed Aunt B's car as a favor to her. Why? I'm confused. I feel like I've walked into a movie halfway through and I don't know who any of the characters are or what their motivations are.

And I've become very attached to one of those characters.

Just slow down, Amy. Don't let your emotions get the better of you. You hardly even know Stoker really. Maybe I'm too attached. These emotions I'm feeling are all new to me and because of that I don't know how to control them properly.

I need to get to know Stoker better, find out what makes him tick.

But if I dig too deep, am I going to find something I don't like?

His relationship with Aunt B is like a closed box I daren't open because I don't think I'll like what I find inside. I know I won't like it. And if he had a relationship with my aunt then that puts a question mark over his relationship with me. Is he trying to relive what he had with her through me? Do I remind him of her and he doesn't like the real me at all, just who I remind him of?

I swivel around in the chair thinking about all these questions and what I should do next. Is there anything I can do? I'm falling for Stoker, I know that. Will my emotions lead me down a path to a place where my heart will be broken?

Something on the wall catches my eye. The watercolor painting of the bookshop that hangs on the wall behind the counter. There's a signature on the bottom right hand corner, painted in black with a flourish.

Dean Stoker.

So he definitely knew Aunt Beth well enough to give her a painting. Not necessarily, maybe she commissioned it. Come on, Amy, don't try and fool yourself. They had some sort of relationship.

Which makes my relationship with him seem very false. In fact, it's fair to say that Dean Stoker is lying to me.

How do I always end up in these situations where

matters of the heart are concerned? All my life I don't feel any spark with anyone and then when a guy comes along who *does* make that spark happen, it's all a lie. It's like a cruel joke. I feel like closing the shop, going home and going to bed and burying my head under the covers.

But I can't do that. I have to keep Promise Books open for Aunt B. It isn't her fault. She never knew any of this was going to happen after she was gone.

So I stay. I sit quietly behind the counter while my mind races over what Detective Macbeth told me and what Stoker *isn't* telling me. It's like everything is going on around me and I'm stuck in the middle of it all just letting it happen.

No more. I can't just sit here and take it. I won't have my emotions flung about like they don't mean anything to anyone.

I storm to the door and flip the sign so it says 'Closed'. I'm not going home to wallow in self-pity; I'm going to Stoker Autos to confront Dean Stoker. I get into the Volvo and gun the engine, almost stalling it as I pull out into the road because I bring the clutch up too fast.

It's time for answers.

And Stoker is going to give them to me.

PART THREE
STORM

BREAK

AMY

I won't cry. I won't. Not until I know the truth about Stoker and my aunt and whether everything he has told me has been a lie. As I get into the Volvo, heavy rain starts to fall from the sky, as if it will shed the tears I refuse to. It bounces off the windshield in big drops and I turn the wipers on as I realize that I don't know the way to Stoker Autos. I know the address but not where it is so I turn on the Volvo's GPS and type in the address. A woman's voice tells me to do a one eighty and turn around. For a moment, I consider doing just that and not confronting Stoker at all. I could just go back to the shop and forget this. Why spoil what we have between us?

But I know that this question, the question of what

exactly happened between Stoker and Aunt B, will haunt me forever if I don't find out the truth. As long as I know the truth, I can handle it and try to deal with it. Not knowing if Stoker is lying to me is eating me up inside.

I follow the GPS instructions out of town and along the road that leads to Stoker Autos. How could he not have told me the police interviewed him about Aunt B's death? That means they actually thought he could be a suspect. And Detective Macbeth's words seemed to suggest that Stoker "made contact" with me to see if he got away with the crime. My own thoughts are along the lines that Stoker had some sort of intimate relationship with Aunt B and is now only with me because I remind him of her.

I see the garage up ahead in the pouring rain and I pull off the road and stop the car in front of the reception door. Rushing in through the door to avoid the rain, I still get soaked immediately. Inside the small reception office, I ring the bell on the counter to get someone's attention.

A man in his fifties comes into the office from the garage. He's wearing blue overalls and his hands are covered in streaks of oil. There's definitely a family resemblance between him and Stoker. This must be Max.

'Can I help you?' he asks, wiping his hands on a rag.

'I'm looking for Stoke…Dean. Is he here?'

He shakes his head. 'He took the afternoon off. It's quiet.'

'Oh. Do you know where he is?'

'The beach maybe. Or Penzance. I'm not sure.'

'Thanks.' I'll call him, find out where he is. I turn for the door.

'Miss?'

'Yes?'

'Are you Beth Anderson's niece?'

'Yes, I am.'

He hesitates as if he's not sure how to follow up his question then says, 'I'm sorry about your aunt.'

'Thank you, Mr Stoker.' I rush across to my car and get in quickly. My hair sticks to my face in long wet tendrils which I push out of my eyes. I'm sure my makeup must be running down my face. Great. Just what I need today on top of everything else. I dial Stoker's number on my phone and he picks up straight away.

'Hey, Amy.'

'Hey.' Will he be able sense the coldness in my voice? I've returned to my usual numb self. I don't want to but the survival mechanism kicked in when I was a little girl and has been with me ever since is protecting me from my emotions. 'Where are you?'

'I came by the bookshop earlier but you were talking to someone so I went for a drive. I'm at the beach. Not working today.'

Talking to someone. Yes, I was talking to Detective, Macbeth, the man who interviewed you about my aunt's death. 'You're at the beach in the rain?'

'I'm sitting in the car.'

'What you doing?'

'Just thinking.'

'About what?'

'You.'

'Oh?'

'Yeah. Are you OK? You sound…I don't know.'

'I need to speak to you, Stoker.'

'Just come to the beach. The one I showed you. Do you know the way?'

'Yes, I think so.'

'I'll see you soon.'

I hang up and start the car. As I pull away from the garage and look in the rearview mirror, I see Max Stoker standing at the window of the reception watching me.

———

The dirt road takes me to the parking area by the secret beach. The last time I was here, I felt so happy being with Stoker and visiting the Cave of the Mermaid with him but now a seed of doubt has been planted in my mind and I can't halt its growth. I don't want to have this conversation with him, I really don't, especially after our relationship leaped forward at Le Chambre but I know this has to be done. I'm hoping Stoker will have answers to my questions that will kill my fears and let us continue on as we have been.

I want that so bad but I've had enough disappointments in my life that I never expect good things to happen. I stop my car next to his and look at him through the rain-streaked window. The wet ribbons of water running down the glass distort his face as he looks at me. My phone buzzes. A text from him.

'My car or yours?'

'Yours,' I reply. If this goes bad and I am in his car, I can just open the door and leave. If he is in my car, I would have to get him to leave. It's easier if I go to his.

I open my door and get into his car as quickly as I can but the rain still drenches me. I close the door. Stoker is wet too. He must have been on the beach when the rain started.

He reaches over and cups my cheek and leans forward. I kiss him but it isn't like before. In the back of my mind I curse Peter Macbeth for ruining what Stoker and I had. It wasn't purposeful but his words and their consequences have ripped me from the only boy who ever made me feel. This just isn't fair.

I break the kiss and sit back in my seat.

He knows something is wrong. It's probably written all over my face. 'What's the matter, Amy?'

'I need to ask you some things.'

'Sounds serious.'

'It may be, Stoker. I don't know. I need you to be truthful with me.'

His own face looks serious now and he sits facing me waiting for my questions.

'You said you came by the bookshop earlier but I was talking to someone. So why didn't you come into the shop? I would have thought you'd come in and wait. Or did you know that the person I was talking to wasn't just a normal customer? You knew who that person was, didn't you?'

He doesn't answer me at first. He looks at the rain droplets rolling down the windshield and seems to be considering what he's going to say.

'I want the truth, Stoker.'

He looks at me and says, 'Yes, I knew who he was. Macbeth.'

'The police detective who interviewed you about my aunt's death.'

'He spoke to me, yes.'

'And you know why he spoke to you?'

He sighs and says, 'Something about an oil stain and a link between me and her.'

'So what is this link?'

'It's nothing, really.'

'Stoker, don't lie to me. You fixed my aunt's car as a favor. Mechanics don't do that as a rule.'

'I liked Beth.'

'How much? How well did you know her?'

'We were friends.'

'Seems like an odd friendship to me.'

'Why? You're a lot like her and *we're* friends. At least I thought we were.'

'What do you mean by that?'

'I mean that you don't have the right to question me like this. It's like an interrogation. You don't trust me?'

'How can I trust you when I find out that there are things you haven't told me? You've been arrested for fighting. You had contact with my aunt that interested the police after she died. You didn't tell me any of that. How can I trust you?' The tears come now, streaming down my face in hot stinging trails.

Stoker leans forward to take me in his arms but I can't have that…I can't have him touching me right now. I open the door and get back in my own car. I sit there crying and I don't even know why. I didn't get the answers I needed and I'm no closer to knowing anything. Stoker's door opens and he comes around to my window, knocking on it with his knuckles. I press the button on the dash that locks the Volvo.

'Amy, let me in.'

Even though I'm crying, I feel the familiar numbness inside. Maybe I'm only crying because I know this situation deserves tears even if they don't have the force of emotion behind them. This isn't right. I should be feeling more pain than this.

'Amy.' Stoker's rapping on the window opens the cuts on his knuckles and his blood turns the rivulets of rainwater red on my window. 'Open the door.'

Somewhere over the sea, lightning flashes followed by the low growl of thunder. The rain hisses off the cars, forming a mist over the paintwork. He shouldn't be out in this. He needs to get back to his car. As long as I'm here, he won't do that.

I start the Volvo.

'Amy, no!'

I reverse and turn the car around so I'm facing back up the dirt road. In the rearview, Stoker is standing next to his car in the hissing rain watching me. I slam the car into first and peel off along the dirt road and the further I get from him the smaller he becomes in the mirror. Eventually he blurs with all the rain streaks and I stop looking in the mirror at all until I hit the main road and I'm on my way to Promise House.

There are things there that can help make me feel.

————

Stoker

I don't know what the fuck just happened.

It was going so well until Macbeth put crazy ideas into Amy's head. Maybe I should go after her. Speak with her. But what could I say that would make any difference to how she feels? She doesn't trust me so anything I say now could be seen as a lie even though I would never do that to Amy.

I hardly feel the rain beating down on me or hear the thunder groaning in the sky behind me. My mind is wrapped up in the situation between Amy and me. I thought she was the girl who could change my life. I only wanted to make her happy. But I've fucked it all up.

I get into the Astra and drive towards the main road. I know where I'm going even though I can't remember deciding I was going to there. I haven't been there for over a year.

Not since the accident.

I don't even know why I'm going there except that somewhere in the depths of my mind I think I may find answers there. Answers to what, I don't know. I don't even know the question.

I arrive there twenty minutes later and now the storm is rolling in from the sea in full force. Angry black clouds cry rain and spit lightning and the wind pummels the grass and trees on the cliff road.

This place seem so innocuous, just a bend in the road. But this is the exact spot that my life took a freefall into tragedy and my mother's and brother's lives were ended.

All because of a loose screw. It turns out that the reason the other driver stopped his car on the road was because he heard a rattling in his engine. So he stopped to investigate. The noise came from a loose screw that had found its way into the engine housing and started rattling about.

Because of that screw, three people died.

Fate can turn on the smallest things sometimes.

I pull off the road into a parking area to stop history repeating itself and I get out into the storm. The wind threatens to blow me off my feet so I lean into it and climb through the hedge onto the grass on the other side by the cliff edge. It's only ten feet from the road to the edge of the cliff, which is why I was thrown all the way over the edge and into the sea below without hitting the ground.

This bend is the only part of this road where that could have happened.

Fate can play the cruellest tricks sometimes.

If I had died along with Mum and James, would it matter? There would be three graves side by side in the Sea Road Cemetery but would anything else be any different?

Dad would be just the same as now, getting drunk every night and pulling old photos out of the shoebox.

If I was dead would he get my photos out too or would he still leave them in the box?

I think I know the answer to that question.

I walk to the edge and look down at the hundred foot drop that saved my life. The seas is deep here. The cliffs angle down into the depths and the only place where the water gets shallow is the rocky are I pulled myself onto fifteen months ago, my wounds stinging from the salt water and the state of shock and the pain making me black out.

The wind coming inland tries to push me away from the edge. I lean into it and step closer to the drop. Everything changed on the day I went over this cliff edge. I stopped being myself and tried to become my dead brother to please Dad. I relegated my own interests to stolen time and secret painting sessions.

Beth could have changed that. She was going to change that. But even then I was worried that Dad would be losing me just as he lost James.

In reality, he lost me a long time ago.

When I went hurtling away from the crash that killed Mum and James and fate decided to throw me over this edge to the sea below, I left my real self in the dark waters. When I crawled onto those rocks, I lost my own identity by trying to be James for Dad. I was denying the fact that my brother was dead. Gone. He was unique. And now he was dead.

I can't love Amy fully unless I'm myself. Dean Stoker. And I do love her. She deserves the real me, not someone who lives a certain way to avoid facing hard truths.

James is dead.

Mum is dead.

I love Amy Anderson.

I shudder against the cold rain and take a step forward so I'm standing on the very edge, the angry water churning a hundred feet below me.

I take a step into nothingness and suddenly the rocky cliff face is speeding past me and I'm falling through the storm towards the sea.

———

Amy

I sit on the bed. A single razor blade glints in the light from the lamp on the nightstand. This will help. This will make me feel.

I pick it up carefully between my thumb and forefinger and hold it up in front of my eyes. My face is reflected in the razor blade, hideously distorted by the metal just as Stoker's face was blurred by the rain. It's hard to know what's real anymore and what is illusion.

Pain.

Pain is real.

I move the wickedly sharp blade to my left arm, the thin edge hovering above the scars. Stoker kissed those scars. He saw them and he wasn't repulsed by me. He made love to me.

Love.

So if I've just broken up with the man I love, I should feel pain. A lot of pain.

I draw the razor across the skin just below my shoulder and I bite my lip at the sharp pain that arcs through my nerves and makes me wince. The blood is warm as it springs from the wound and trickles down my arm. A single tear rolls down my cheek.

Outside, thunder rolls heavily across the evening sky, shaking Promise House.

I position the blade lower, over my bicep. I need more pain.

———

Stoker

The water is like concrete, knocking the breath out of me when I hit it. I exhale as I go under, my lungs emptying of air as the force of my fall takes me down...down... down into the depths. The last time I was here in this water everything was calm. There was no storm then. Now, the surface is choppy with waves. At the moment that is irrelevant though because the surface is far above me and an undercurrent is dragging me further away from it.

I struggle against the irresistible pull of the current, flailing my arms and legs uselessly. I barely have any breath in my lungs. I know what will happen of I don't get to the surface soon. Blackout. Drowning. Death.

Would it be so bad? Maybe this is what was supposed to happen fifteen months ago. Maybe I've been living on borrowed time and the grim reaper has brought me back here to take what is rightfully his.

No, I can't die.

Amy.

I love Amy.

I stop struggling against the sea and I feel its rhythm moving all around me. Back and forth. Currents pulsing like a metronome.

Instead of resisting, I kick out gently with the movement of the current, using a sweeping motion of my arms to propel my body upward. Two more strokes from my arms and I break the surface of the water, my lungs pulling in oxygen.

I let the waves take me towards the rocky shore and when I get there, I climb out of the sea. Lying on the rocks, I regain my breath and wait for the warmth to return to my body.

I'm alive.

Amy

I hesitate, the edge of the razor blade pressed against my skin. I've never known a storm like this. It hits the house and shakes it, rattling the windows. I'm about to go ahead and cut again when I think of Mr Tibbles. I haven't seen him since I got home. Surely he isn't out in this weather. Cats hate rain and storms and he has his cat flap so I'm sure he's in the house. So why haven't I seen him? Probably hiding somewhere.

I try to return to the business at hand but I can't stop thinking about the cat. I have to know he's safe. Stoker and I brought the cat from Penzance together and I have to make sure the cat is OK. I don't try to rationalize it.

'Mr Tibbles?' I call out. I listen for a meow or the sound of his paws on the stairs but the rain and thunder make it hard to hear anything else.

I'm not going to be able to do anything else until I know he's OK so I wrap a bandage around the cut in my left arm and go out into the hallway. 'Here kitty. Mr Tibbles.' From somewhere downstairs, I hear a sad meow.

So he's inside but he sounds like he's in pain or distress.

I go down to the hallway. 'Mr Tibbles? You here?'

Another cry. This time I can locate it as coming from the living room. I go in there and get to my knees, peering under the sofa to see a huge pair of green eyes staring back at me.

'Mr Tibbles, you scaredy cat.'

He starts to purr but stays where he is. I can't coax him out no matter how much I talk to him.

I don't feel like going back upstairs just yet. I want to call Stoker. I made a mistake not trusting him earlier. What is in the past is in the past. I can't keep living my life looking backward all the time. I just wish I'd handled the confrontation in his car better. He was right to tell me to stop questioning him. I can't just interrogate him like that.

I hear a noise outside and headlights sweep through

the window as someone pulls onto the driveway. I go to the window and my heart leaps when I see Stoker's car. Running to the doorway, I fix my hair and clothing as best I can.

I hear him step onto the porch and I open the door. When I see him, I gasp, my hand going to my heart. 'Stoker!'

He leans against the doorframe, his eyes half-closed. He is absolutely soaked to the skin. His hair hangs down in his eyes. He's dripping water everywhere and at first I think it's from when he was standing out in the rain but he smells like the sea. Why the hell would he be in the sea? He staggers forward and I keep him upright by holding onto his jacket. He feels so cold.

'Come on,' I say, 'this way.' I lead him into the living room and tell him to remove his clothes while I build a fire and get blankets. I bundle logs and fire starters into the fireplace and light the arrangement with a match. Stoker struggles out of his clothes and I fetch him a towel from the downstairs bathroom. As he dries himself, I rush upstairs for blankets off one of the spare beds. By the time I get back down to him, he's curled up on the sofa, eyes closed.

I lay the blankets over him and put his clothes out by the fire and wonder if I should take him to a hospital. How the hell did he get in this state? I don't rule out the hospital but I put it on the back burner for now. He just seems wet and cold and tired. Despite his condition, it's so good to see him again.

I don't want to leave him so instead of going up to bed,

I get a blanket for myself and sit on the rug in front of the fire, leaning against the easy chair. Stoker sleeps peacefully, his breathing deep and slow, his body still.

Watching him makes me sleepy myself and I feel my eyes drooping shut. I let myself fall asleep.

All thoughts of the razor upstairs are gone.

TORN

AMY

I wake up the next morning to find Stoker sitting on the sofa watching me. He's still naked and he has the blankets wrapped around him.

'How are you feeling?' I ask.

He runs a hand through his hair. 'Not bad considering.'

'Considering what?' It feels good to be talking to him again.

'Considering I took a dive into the sea last night.'

'Stoker, why? I don't understand.'

'I'm not so sure I understand myself. I don't know what came over me. I went to the place where the accident happened. I looked over the cliff to where I was thrown into the sea and I remember thinking that I changed when

I came crawling out of the water that day. I changed for the worst. I wanted to change back, to become who I used to be again. It was stupid and I paid the price.'

'You can't turn back time, Stoker.'

'I know. If I could do that, I would have been more open and honest with you from the beginning. Then you wouldn't get mad at me and take my paintings off the wall.'

'What? What do you mean? I hung the painting you gave me in the kitchen. It's still there.'

He points at the wall behind the sofa. 'No, I mean the two paintings that were hanging there.'

I look at the wall blankly.

He says, 'A watercolor of the lighthouse at Pendeen and a colored pencil sketch of the beach at Porthcurno.'

I shake my head. I don't know what he's talking about. He sees my confusion and says, 'OK, look…there was nothing going on between Beth and me. Not in the way you think anyway. The paintings that were hanging there on the wall and the one in the bookshop were bought and paid for. I sold them to her. She loved my work and said I would be successful some day. Your aunt was my patron. She bought me some materials and she bought my work and she said she was going to fund me to take an art course at a college in Manchester. I was going to pay her back of course and I was working extra shifts at the garage to get some money together but I don't get paid much. As far as my dad is concerned, he provides the roof over my head and I don't need much else.'

My mind is working on the puzzle, remembering Aunt

B's words. Look for what doesn't fit. Mr Tibbles in the cattery didn't fit. These missing paintings don't fit. The cat fits my suicide theory. The paintings don't. What do the paintings mean? Theft? Why would anyone steal the work of an unknown artist? No, there are much more valuable pieces of art hanging on the walls of Promise House. So if it's not theft, then why would Aunt B remove the paintings herself?

My mind starts piecing it together slowly. Maybe the fact that Mr Tibbles was in a cattery in Penzance doesn't mean what I thought it meant…that Aunt B was planning to take her own life. Maybe he was in a cattery for the most likely reason of all; his owner was going away. And he was in Penzance because if she was going somewhere via Penzance and returning via Penzance, picking him up there on the way back would be easy. She wouldn't be going out of her way because she would be driving by there anyway.

I get up and go get the car keys. Stoker says, 'Hey, wait for me. Where are you going?'

'You should stay here, you aren't wearing any clothes,' I remind him. 'I'm not going anywhere. Back in a minute.' I slip my shoes on because even though it isn't raining anymore, the ground is wet I go out to the Volvo, get in and turn in the ignition but don't start the car. I press the button the the dash that activates the GPS and scroll through the history of locations Aunt B has put into the navigation system. The top address tells me everything I need to know.

College of the Arts, Manchester.

So Aunt B was going to the college in Manchester. She made arrangements for her cat, taking him to Meow Meow the day before she left so she could collect him as she drove south from Manchester on he return. She must have planned to go other places while she was up north because the GPS has other addresses around that area programmed into it.

And that explains the paintings. She was taking them to the college as examples of Stoker's work. I take the keys and go around to the trunk and open it. Empty. Damn.

I go back and open the glove compartment. She must have been taking some paperwork with her. Also empty.

Still a little confused, I go back inside to find a fully-dressed Stoker coming out to meet me. 'What's going on?' he asks.

'Did Aunt B mention she was going away?'

'No, she just told me she needed her car and I had to have it back to her the next morning. She didn't say she was going away.'

'Oh my God, her car broke down.'

'Her exhaust fell off.'

'And you towed her car to your garage. Macbeth told me he saw it there.'

Stoker nods.

'But you didn't take it back to her the next morning because you heard that her body had been found on the beach.'

He looks down sadly. 'That's right.'

'Stoker, I know my aunt and whenever she goes away, she always packs the car the day before so she can set off straight away on the morning of her journey without having to worry about it.'

He shrugs. 'OK.'

'So why isn't her luggage in the car? Why aren't the paintings in there? There must have been some paperwork she had to take with her, if only a letter they sent her.'

He frowns at me as if I've gone crazy. 'Amy, I'm not following you. What paperwork? And why would my paintings be in her car?'

'I think she was planning on going to the at college in Manchester. It's programmed into her GPS. I know her, Stoker, she would have put the paintings, the paperwork and her luggage in the car the day before. The day she took Mr Tibbles to the Meow Meow cattery. Then on the way back to Promise Cove, on the Sea Road, her car broke down.'

A thought enters my mind which chills me to the bone. I don't want my fear to be confirmed but I have to know. 'Tell me about what happened when you took her car to your garage.'

'Nothing out of the ordinary. She rang me on my mobile and I took the Land Rover out there, hooked up the Volvo, dropped your aunt here at the house and took the car to the garage.'

'But you didn't fix it right away.' It isn't a question. I'm starting to see links and the whole dark story is unfolding in my mind.

'No, I had to go out on another call to tow a Nova which had a broken steering shaft.'

'And when you came back later and fixed my aunt's tailpipe, did you open the trunk?'

He nods. 'I gave the car a clean inside and out. That includes the boot.'

'And it was empty,' I say to myself. I don't know how I'm going to tell him what I think happened to Aunt B. How will he react? Could I be mistaken?

'Just a few bits and pieces. Nothing weird. Certainly no paintings or luggage.'

'Stoker, did your father know about Aunt B funding you to go to cart college?'

'Hell no! He knew nothing about it. I was going to tell him eventually but not until it was definitely going to happen. I told you what he thinks about that stuff.'

'He killed her, Stoker. He killed my aunt.'

'What? That's crazy.'

'He looked in the car and he found your paintings and the letter from the college. He knew where Aunt B was headed. If he didn't take the paintings from the car then where are they?'

'Amy, you don't know for sure they were there in the first place.'

I point the wall where they used to hang. 'So where are they?'

He can't answer that.

'The last thing I want to do is hurt you, Stoker, but you have to see there's no other explanation.'

He stares at the wall. 'I don't believe it. I can't. He wouldn't do something like that. I know him.'

I know he doesn't want to believe it of his own father

but Aunt Beth's mantra of looking for what doesn't fit has convinced me. 'Tell me more about that night…the night Aunt Beth died. Was your father with you all that night?'

He shakes his head. 'I went out at about ten in the Land Rover. Just for a drive to the secret cove. It was a lovely night and I sat there on the beach for a while. I didn't know that a little further up the coast…' He breaks off and exhales a long sigh. 'Amy, I can't believe what you're implying.'

'I think you may have suspected this yourself, Stoker. I'm saying your father could be a murderer and you're taking it very well. You aren't angry about it or shouting or upset.'

He throws his arms up and looks at me with a sadness in his gray eyes. 'When I heard about Beth, I admit that the thought did cross my mind. Dad didn't hate her as a person but he hated that she was encouraging me in a direction he didn't want me to take. But this…even Dad wouldn't…I don't know.'

I touch his arm gently, feeling the tight hard muscles beneath his clothes. I don't want to hurt him. It's the last thing I want in the world.

'There's something else,' he says. 'The day after your aunt died is when I discovered the scratch on the front of the Astra. It wasn't there the day before. The only explanation is that Dad took the car out that night.'

I take his hand in both of mine. 'Maybe we should call Detective Macbeth.'

He thinks about that for a moment then shakes his head slowly. 'What we're saying…it's all circumstantial. I can't go to the police without being certain we're right. If we're wrong, he'll never forgive me. I can't take that chance.'

'I understand, Stoker. But you need to know that I won't let this go. My aunt is dead. I can't turn my back on her.'

'I agree. That's why we're going go to the garage right now.'

'What? Why? I don't think confronting your dad is…'

'No, we're going to have a look around the back. That's where Beth's car was parked when I went out on the Nova job. If my paintings were in the car as you say then they must be there somewhere.'

'What about your dad? I don't think he likes me, Stoker. He won't want me snooping around his place.'

He reaches out and touches my cheek. I wonder if he knows what his touch does to me. 'You'll be with me, Amy. Everything will be fine. I won't let anything happen to you.'

I nod. I do feel safe with him. He's strong and manly and protective and being with him makes me feel both complete and secure.

We leave the house and get in the Astra and drive to Stoker Autos.

If what I believe is right then we are about to face a murderer.

———

Stoker drives the car around the back of the garage. It's like junkyard back here and the broken carcasses of vehicles sit rotting in the sun. We stop among them and get out of the Astra. 'Beth's car was parked over there,' Stoker says pointing to a clear area next to the building. 'If what you say is correct then he would have hidden the paintings somewhere around here. He couldn't put them in the garage or the house because I'd see them. They're quite large. So unless he destroyed them, he would have put them here.'

We search the area, looking in the broken car windows and underneath the rusting hulks for Stoker's paintings.

As I peer into the cracked rear window of a Honda, I can't help thinking that these rotten shells were once brand new cars, someone's pride and joy. Now they are broken and twisted and forgotten. Is this how our lives play out? Sometimes I feel like I'm cracked and twisted like these wrecks but meeting Stoker has helped me heal. I feel so bad that we could uncover something now that will tear his family apart even further.

He walks over to me and I can see by his face that he isn't happy.

'I found them,' he says.

He points to a smashed silver Toyota and I can see the paintings sticking out of the open trunk. A watercolor of a lighthouse and a pencil drawing of a beach. The canvasses are torn, the paintings destroyed.

'Oh my God, Stoker, I'm so sorry.'

'There was this too.' He hands me a piece of paper. It's a letter from a college in Manchester confirming Aunt

Beth's appointment with them regarding Dean Stoker and telling her to bring the letter and examples of his work with her when she visits. The visit is scheduled for the day after she was killed.

Killed.

Not suicide.

Murder.

Stoker breaks down. He fall to his knees in front of the destroyed paintings and bows his head and cries. I go to him and kneel next to him, placing my hand across his back but not knowing what to say. There's nothing I can say. So I do the only thing I can for him right now and try to give him my support. No one deserves what he has gone through, his family totally ripped into pieces and scattered to the wind.

'Dean?'

I freeze when I hear the voice of Max Stoker calling from beyond the cars.

'Dean, are you there?' Closer now. He's coming this way.

I feel Stoker's muscles tense beneath my touch and he fists his hands tightly as he stands up. 'Over here,' he calls out. His voice is full of tension and I'm afraid of what he's going to do when his father reaches us. There's the sound of footfalls getting closer then Max Stoker appears and walks toward us. He must know why we're here. His face looks twisted into a mixture of worry and anger.

'What have you done?' Stoker says, taking a step toward his father.

'Stoker, be careful,' I whisper. I don't know if he can hear me or not anymore.

Max Stoker looks at his son and says, 'I was just trying to give you a dose of reality. Chasing these stupid dreams isn't going to get you anywhere in life.'

'I don't mean the paintings. I'm talking about Beth Anderson. This isn't about the paintings.'

'Of course it's about the paintings! How do you think I felt seeing those paintings and reading that letter. First your mother and brother leave me and now you're planning to abandon me too.'

'They didn't leave you, Dad, they were killed. And I'm allowed to live my own life.'

'Your own life? Painting? Is that it? You want to sit on your ass all day and paint? Why can't you be a man like your brother?'

'I'm not James.'

'Oh, you've got that right. He was going to be successful, make something of his life. While you…you just want to throw yours away.'

'Is that why you killed her?'

'Killed who? That woman who filled your head with useless dreams? I didn't kill her.' He hesitates a moment. 'She fell.'

'I know you were there.'

'Of course I was there. I'm not going to let her steal my son away. I went to give her a piece of my mind, tell her to stay away from you. What makes her think she can be your parent? I'm your parent.'

'Yes, you are my parent. A bad parent.'

'Well what do you expect when you don't act like a proper man? You let these women fill your head with nonsense. First Beth Anderson and now her niece. I'll be a proper parent when you're a proper son.'

'What did you do to Beth?' Stoker asks through clenched teeth.

'She tried to ignore me, Dean. Went walking past me to that big house of hers and she ignored me. She was going to help you go away, leave me. I told her to turn and face me and when she did, I got so angry I pushed her. Not hard. Just a push. If she'd fallen over where she stood, that would have been the end of it but she stumbled backwards and tried to keep on her feet. Why didn't she just drop to the ground? She would have been safe if she just dropped to the ground but she kept going, tripping backward. Over the edge.' Tears spring up in his eyes and I feel the same thing happening in my own eyes. I loved Aunt Beth. I can't believe that this man killed her because she was helping his son achieve his dreams.

Stoker lashes out. His fist connects with his father's face and the older man goes down spitting blood from a cut lip. He looks up at his son from the ground and smiles a bloody smile. 'At least you won't be going away to college now. You won't be leaving me, Dean. Don't leave me like your mum and James left me.'

Stoker stands over him, his fist bleeding and says, 'I won't be who you want me to be anymore.' He looks at me and says, 'Call Detective Macbeth.'

———

After the endless questions from the police and giving signed statements in the Penzance police station, we get back to Promise House at dusk. The sea is calm and a low pale orange glow makes the sky seem like its made of burning embers.

I lead Stoker inside the house and up to the bedroom without a word, holding his hand as I take him to the bed. He sees the need in my eyes and I see the same in his. It's like his soul has been laid bare and I can see into it through a window in his intense eyes.

My own soul has taken a beating too. Finding out that Aunt B was murdered makes me feel her loss more keenly. She was taken from this world before her time and at the hands of another human being driven by a tragedy that is similar to the tragedy that seems to touch all our lives.

'Stoker, I need you.'

He nods and dips his head so our lips meet. I've missed kissing him so much and when I taste him again it feels like coming home. His hands go to my hips and pull at the hem of my t-shirt. I lift my arms and we break the kiss for a moment as he lifts it over my head.

'And yours,' I whisper.

He removes his own shirt and my hands go to his muscular torso, feeling the smooth hard muscles beneath my fingers. Stoker reaches behind me and unhooks my bra. I shrug out of it and his hands go to my breasts, squeezing them softly while his thumbs flick over my nipples, making me squirm with pleasure. His mouth replaces his hands and he is licking me hotly, sucking the sensitive points of my breasts into his mouth and teasing them with his tongue. I run my fingers through his hair at the back of his head and over his strong shoulders.

He pushes me down to the bed, his mouth trailing down over my stomach to the edge of my jeans. I feel hot and wet and out of control and I need him to experience me in the most intimate way possible. I lift my hips as he pulls down my jeans and panties and I'm totally exposed to him. His mouth closes over me and I arch my back, gasping his name as his tongue explores my most intimate place. The sensations tingling through my body explode into over drive and suddenly I'm crying out as everything clenches with a delicious bolt of pleasure and I'm being thrown into the whirling vortex of an orgasm.

I lay there shuddering while Stoker removes his jeans and takes a condom from his wallet. He looks so hard and strong as he puts it on and I want him inside me so badly. I need this close contact with him. I need to feel a connection with him and I know he needs the same thing.

He props himself above me on his powerful arms and looks into my eyes as I feel him seeking entrance to my body. I allow him inside and we both gasp at the sudden pleasure-filled union.

'Amy,' he whispers as he buries himself deep within me. His eyes close and he gasps with the sensation of feeling me tight around him and I am so glad that I can give him this feeling, this joy.

He arches his back and throws his head back and cries out my name again as he loses control and twitches deep within me.

CHAPTER
FOURTEEN

RESTORE

AMY

I hold the books close to my chest as I push open the doors with my butt and walk out into the sunshine. It's only Spring and there's a slight chill in the air but anything is better than being stuck inside when the sun is shining. Besides, I need to take some more photos for my course work.

The campus of Manchester School of Art is quiet today with only a few students milling around. I sit on one of the benches and adjust the camera strap that seems to be biting into my shoulder. I check my watch. Stoker said he'd meet me here at twelve and take me for lunch. He's typically late.

I guess I should check up on the shop. I find my phone in my bag and hit the button.

'Promise Books, how may I help you?'

'Dell, it's me. How are things going?'

'Hey, all is good. How's college life treating ya?'

'Fine. I'm just waiting for Stoker to meet me for lunch.'

'Coolio. When are you two going to come down to Promise Cove for a weekend, hmm? Mr Tibbles misses you both.'

'Mr Tibbles, huh?'

'Well, OK, I miss you both too. But it's mainly the cat. He never stops meowing.'

'We'll be down soon, I promise.'

'Great because I need your advice on something.'

'What?'

'The Macbeth issue.'

'There isn't a Macbeth issue.'

'I've seen the way he looks at me. Believe me, there's a Macbeth issue.'

'Dell, what the hell have you done?'

'Nothing. He's just been coming in here most days buying up all the crime novels. And I've noticed things. Like he always tips me and he looks at me with those intense blue eyes.'

'You sure you're not imagining it?'

'Hey, I'm the most grounded person you know. Anyway, got to go…you know who is here. Don't worry about anything; the house and store and cat are fine. We're all fine.' She hangs up.

'Who was that?'

I whirl round to see Stoker standing behind me. 'Just Dell.'

He snakes an arm around my waist and pulls me to him, kissing me for what seems like an eternity of delicious sensation.

'Mmm, I can get used to that,' I say as we break. 'You have a dab of paint on you just here,' I thumb away a green oil paint mark on his cheek.

'Now how about this lunch?' he asks.

'Let's go.' We walk together arm in arm.

'How's Dell?'

'She's great. She thinks Detective Macbeth might have taken a shine to her.'

He laughs. 'That's Dell alright.'

'She also said we should go down there one weekend.'

He thinks about that for a moment then nods. 'Sure, why not? We can visit the Cave of the Mermaid.'

'You trying to drown me, Mister?'

'Hey, I can't help it if you can't swim.

We reach my car and I get into the driver's seat while he gets in the passenger. I put the car into reverse and back out of my space in the lot. Every time I drive I remember that it was Stoker who taught me to use a stick shift. And it was him who made me feel for the first time. And it was because of him that I stopped cutting myself.

A month after the conviction of Max Stoke for the murder of Beth Anderson, I threw away all my blades. I don't need them anymore.

I'm feeling plenty these days and it's all thanks to Dean Stoker. The emotional walls have come crumbling down and the girl who who felt only numbness has become a woman whose new emotions surprise her every day.

I love Stoker and he loves me and that makes my heart swell every time I think about it.

Stoker snaps his fingers in front of my face. 'You OK, Amy? You phased out there for a second. You're not falling asleep, are you?'

I grin and slam the car into first gear.

I feel awake for the first time in my life.

THE END

I hope you enjoyed Amy and Stoker's story. Please remember to leave a review!

Tabi